I0727166

Stone Sentinel:

A Paranormal Protector Tale

Book 3 in the Heart of Steel series

DEMELZA CARLTON

This book was created with the assistance of a grant from the Western Australian Department of Local Government, Sport and Cultural Industries.

ONE

Effie's scream lanced through Wystan's heart. It wasn't the first, but by God and the devil, it would be her last.

"You're killing her!" he shouted as he threw open the cottage door.

"Mr Steel, a birth is no place for a man," the midwife chided, not even looking at him as she pointed outside. "Out!"

"But she's been screaming like this all day. This canna be normal!" Wystan argued, standing his ground.

"This would not be the first bairn to take a day or even two to make their way into the world. Mr Steel…"

Effie's eyes had hell in them. "Another day of this? Oh, I cannot bear it. It hurts so!"

Wystan seized her hands and dropped to his knees beside the bed. "I will find the doctor for you, Euphemia, I swear it. I'll fetch him and bring him right back here to see to you and the bairn. I promise." He pressed his lips to hers for only a moment before he scrambled to his feet. "Just hold on a little longer until I return, Effie." He bolted out the door, as her next scream gave his boots wings.

TWO

When Wystan returned, the cottage was eerily silent. Effie and the bairn must be asleep, he decided, opening the door as quietly as he could. The midwife had been right and they hadn't needed a doctor, which was probably a good thing, for once Wystan had finally found the man, flirting with Carline Steel as he ate dinner with the girl's brother in the grand house on the hill, the uppity bastard had refused to come.

Ah, there she was, stretched out on the bed, fast asleep, with the swaddled baby sleeping on her breast. They were both exhausted from their ordeal. He did not wish to wake them, so he'd sleep on a pallet by the fire tonight.

Except…no fire had been lit, though it was nearly dark. Perhaps Effie had been too tired to even stoke the fire, so it had gone out.

He might not have been able to bring the doctor, but he could light a decent fire to keep his family warm when they woke up. Perhaps he could even put on a pot of stew to simmer while they slept…

His cousins would laugh if they knew he cooked more than Effie did. Effie could prepare meat and vegetables and even bread, but when it came time to cook anything…she just got so caught up in her sewing or whatever else she was doing that she forgot. Either she forgot to cook things or she forgot things were cooking, so everything came out either raw or burned. If Wystan wanted something in between, he'd had to take matters into his own hands.

Just as he would tonight, so there'd be something for Effie to eat when she woke. Then again, maybe he should wait until morning, for if he lit the lantern to see by, he'd surely wake her, when she needed sleep after labouring so long to bring their first child into the world. He'd make her breakfast in the morning, he told himself.

But before he lay down on his pallet by the now crackling fire, he couldn't resist giving Effie a good night kiss.

He leaned over the bed, brushing a stray lock of hair off her face, before he planted both hands on either side of her head.

The moment his lips touched hers, he knew something was wrong. Never, not even on the iciest winter's day, had her lips ever felt so cold. Nor could he feel her breath, and when he felt for the pulse he'd always felt beat so strongly at her throat…

Nothing.

Hardly daring to breathe, he reached for the swaddled bairn…

Only to howl his grief into the night, for he'd lost everything.

THREE

Years had passed, and he was half a world away, but as Wystan waited in the dark with Grant and Harlow while Stan crept through the bush to steal a bride for himself, that night he'd found Effie and his daughter dead might have been yesterday, the grief still felt that fresh.

Or perhaps it was dread, that this night held death once more.

"No, wait!" he hissed, but he was too slow. Grant charged out into the open.

A moment later, the boom of a rifle dropped him.

Harlow let out a strangled cry, maddened by grief Wystan knew all too well, as he ran to his brother. Another boom and he fell, too.

First his wife and child, and now his cousins. Wystan had no family left. No one left to live for. He rose to his feet, spreading his arms wide like Christ on the cross in the church back in Scotland, where he'd hung above Effie's coffin on the day of her funeral. On the day he'd buried all his hopes and dreams of a future.

The first shot took him in the shoulder, blasting away a chunk of his arm. Wystan welcomed the pain. The second shot followed the first, until he could no longer feel his arm. Maybe it was gone. The third shot stole his breath as his entire throat felt like it was on fire.

But only for a moment.

By the time his body hit the dirt of the Swan River shore, Wystan was already dead.

But fate wasn't finished with him yet.

FOUR

Tacey knew she should just get going, but she slowed as she reached Callie's new gargoyle statue. How she'd carried the monstrous thing into the house, Tacey had no idea. Maybe he wasn't actually stone? Almost without thinking, she reached around to squeeze what she had to admit was a perfectly sculpted butt cheek. It felt warm and hard, like stone that had been in the sun, but it also had a little give to it, like that special foam Rochelle had used when she made her cosplay armour. So if he was actually foam instead of stone, she should be able to push it into Callie's room so Rory didn't come home to see the monster in all his naked glory.

Yet when she gave him an experimental push, he didn't move at all. She put her full weight to him, shoving against his side because Callie would not forgive her if she broke off that enormous dick, but he didn't budge. Maybe he was stone, and he was just warm because he'd been standing in the sun.

"You'd better hide him before I get home from dinner, Callie," she muttered as she headed for the front door. She did not want to spend her evening explaining penises to a six-year-old.

Of course, Rory wouldn't be Rory if she didn't want Tacey to explain something.

"Mum, who's One Direction? Grandma said you loved them. I thought you were only allowed to love one man, not five. How can you love five men?"

For a moment, Tacey wished she could explain stone penises instead.

She took a deep breath. "They were a band when I was in high school, sweetie. I loved their music, not them. I never met any of them. I only saw them on TV. Kind of like you love the Mandalorian."

"But I want to marry the Mandalorian. You can't marry all five men. Then I'd have five daddies, and you said even one daddy is more than we need. We don't have enough bedrooms for five of them."

Tacey looked askance at her mother.

Mum shrugged. "She was looking for more drawing paper in your desk, and found a stack of your One Direction posters. I took them off the wall, but I didn't throw them away, in case you still wanted them, so when she came to ask me about them, I told her."

"Well, you can safely throw them away now. While I might not turn Harry down if he ever asked me, I doubt there's any chance of me meeting, let alone marrying any of them.

Especially if Rory's going to want astronaut training so she can fly her own spaceship in the future, just like the Mandalorian." Tacey ruffled Rory's hair.

Rory reared back, horrified. For a moment, Tacey thought she might actually bite her – something she hadn't done since she was a toddler. "Mummy! Will you buy me a spaceship, too? When I'm all grown up and a bounty hunter?"

Tacey's mum's eyes grew wide. "That does not sound appropriate."

Oh, not again. "Then you should tell that to Octavia, not me. She's the one who got Rory into Star Wars and all the spinoffs." But Mum would never believe Octavia could be at fault. She believed she'd brought up Octavia too perfectly for that.

"You could always move back home so we can help you take care of her. You could go to university like your sister and make something of yourself," Mum began hopefully.

She'd better shut down that train of thought

before Mum got any further. Tacey shook her head. "No, Mum, I'm fine running the café and living in Bell House with the other girls. It's lovely of you to have Rory over for a sleepover occasionally, but this is the life I want. I'm not Octavia."

Perfect Octavia, the second child they'd done everything right with, after messing up with her. Her parents had never said it aloud, but Tacey knew they'd thought it. If they knew half the things Octavia had done, both while she'd still lived at home and now she'd moved out…but she'd rather let Mum believe the pretty lie than betray Octavia's trust.

"But now Octavia's out working so much, she doesn't have time to help you take care of Rory. If you moved back home…" Mum began hopefully.

"Rory's at school five days a week now, Mum. And Octavia's only working a temporary contract. When it's finished, she'll be back working at the café with me in between developing the game she's working on."

"If she wasn't helping you so much, maybe she'd have finished that game of hers and sold it for millions to some gaming company. You can't rely on your sister's help for everything, Tacita Bell. She does have her own life to live, you know."

As if Octavia would ever let Tacey stand in the way of her ambitions. Octavia had picked out the property where they'd opened the café because of the perfect studio upstairs. Tacey insisted she work the occasional shift in the café – paid, of course, because she wasn't that stingy – in exchange for free rent upstairs, and Octavia had instantly agreed. If Octavia wanted to change the agreement, she only had to ask. As it was, Tacey had had to ask Octavia's permission if Rochelle could stay there while Octavia was working at the mine site up north. If it had been anyone but Rochelle, Octavia probably wouldn't have allowed it, but they'd been friends at university, working together on some secret film project with Rochelle's bloodsucker of an ex-boyfriend. Until he'd hit it big with his video streaming channel, and left the girls to finish the project without any help from him.

Rochelle was much better off with Ben, in Tacey's opinion.

"Are you listening to me, Tacita Bell?" Mum demanded.

"Yes, Mum," Tacey lied.

Mum rolled her eyes. She might not have been the perfect mother – and as a mother herself, Tacey wasn't sure if anyone could actually claim that title – but she knew when Tacey wasn't telling the truth. "Come set the table for dinner. Aurora helped prepare it, you know."

Rory picked exactly that moment to start listening to their conversation. "Don't call me that! That's a princess name! I am not some silly princess! I'm going to be the best bounty hunter in the galaxy, and I can bring you in warm or…"

Well, that was one way to stop Mum in her

tracks. Calming Rory down took the better part of twenty minutes, during which time dinner nearly burned, and by the time the food was all safely on the table, if a little more well done than usual, Mum had completely forgotten about the lecture she'd wanted to deliver.

Thank goodness.

FIVE

Wystan woke in darkness, feeling for all the world like he was a boy again, back in a river full of eels. Everything around him squirming so much he could scarcely feel the icy water at all. Then he burst through the surface, and realised why: he hadn't been in the water, merely mud. And the thrashing, squirming creatures surrounding him were not eels, but men, much like himself.

Until they unfolded their wings and took flight.

Help protect us. HELP.

Wystan wasn't sure if the words floated on the wind or whether they were echoing inside his own head, but he could not refuse the pull. He, too, unfolded his wings and took to the air.

Wait…he had wings?

He twisted in the air, trying to see the great flapping things, and almost fell out of the sky. The ground came up so fast, it took some serious flapping and a swoop that he felt in the depths of his belly to keep him from crashing. The others were so far ahead of him, there'd be nothing left for him to do when he reached her.

And it was a woman. He'd never been able to resist a feminine cry for help, even when there was nothing he could do. He had to try. Could not face himself in the mirror if he didn't at least try.

Finally, he caught up with the others —

perched on the flat top of an enormous tower. He'd have said it was the biggest tower he'd ever seen, but as the words left his lips, they'd have been lies, for this tower didn't stand alone. No, it was one of many – all built close together, of differing sizes, with more windows than walls up the sides, all reflecting the lights lining the streets below.

Like Glasgow, only writ large, larger than he'd ever believed possible. He squinted at the lights below. One large panel proclaimed that the premises were a café, established in 2002.

So this was what happened when a city grew for more than a hundred years. He slept in darkness. The city grew upward and outward, while Wystan grew wings.

Yet even as he approached the top of the tower, he could feel the pull, moving away from him. The woman who needed help wasn't here.

He could not let her pass out of his reach. He had only one purpose, and it was to protect her. Even if she ran from him. He had to catch her, even if she moved impossibly fast.

"Then fly faster," he told himself, as the others set off to follow the same thread tugging at him. A thread that tugged deep within his chest, tied tightly around his heart.

SIX

Tacey found herself in the kitchen, loading the dishwasher, when Mum cornered her again. "I do worry about you girls in that house all alone. I'd feel so much safer if you had a man about the place, or even a big, fierce dog. Your father knows someone who breeds those pit bull things that make good guard dogs. Perhaps if you spoke to him…"

"Mum, we're fine, and you know the lease

conditions for Bell House don't allow men to live there. Women only. Besides, we have Callie, and she's scarier than any man I know. Did I tell you what happened to the last guy she dated? He spent half of their date texting on his phone, then was rude to the waitress, so she changed the language on his phone to Ancient Egyptian while he was in the bathroom. After she set his phone to the silent, do not disturb mode. Oh, and the kitchen accidentally made his meal extra spicy, so his eyes and nose were streaming so bad by the end of the date, he didn't even notice when she left. If anyone dares cross Callie, the whole universe conspires to punish him." Tacey had a horrible thought – what if the gargoyle statue had once been a real man who'd turned to stone? Callie said magic and witchcraft didn't exist, but the way she went around threatening to curse people, Tacey had never been sure what to believe. Then there'd been that demon summoning ritual in the cemetery. Probably for the best the security guard had interrupted them, because she'd definitely felt something happening. If they'd managed to complete the spell, who knows what would have happened? Would a real, actual demon have appeared? What would they have done if it had?

Mum was shaking her head. "Are you talking about your cousin Callie? The one who works at the university, and hasn't grown a centimetre since she was twelve? Matt would break her in two without even blinking to get to you."

Tacey sighed. "Mum, Matt's in prison, where he belongs. He's probably having a bad enough time there without even one of Callie's curses."

Mum's mouth dropped open. "You mean you haven't heard? He got some fancy new lawyer, who appealed his sentence, and he's been released. Cleared of all charges. It's been all over the news."

This time, Tacey's jaw dropped. "You can't be serious. He hasn't even served half his sentence. He's not even up for parole until…until Rory's finished primary school!"

Mum shook her head. "He's been all over the news, saying how justice has been served. He's a lot bigger now, after all his time in prison. Like a bodybuilder."

Tacey shuddered. Matt had always been into sports, but not bulking up muscle. Maybe he'd needed to do it to survive in prison. And here she'd been hoping he'd become some bikie's bitch and…now he was free?

For one crazy moment, she wished Callie's spell in the cemetery had actually worked, so she could borrow Alethea's demon protector to stand guard outside her house.

Then she shook herself. Matt didn't even know where she lived. It's not like he'd be lying in wait for her on the front doorstep.

At least that's what she told herself.

She dried her hands on a tea towel, forcing out a calm smile for her mother's benefit. "Thanks for dinner, Mum, and for taking care of Rory. I should probably get her home now." She stepped into the lounge, where Rory was deliberately ignoring the Disney cartoons in favour of the Lego spread across the rug. Of course she was building some sort of space ship. "C'mon, Rory. Time to go home."

Rory jumped to her feet. "Can we take the Lego with us so I can finish building my ship?"

"No, the Lego has to stay here with Grandma. She'll take good care of your ship, and it'll be here waiting for you when you come back."

Rory pouted, but she came readily enough. "I guess I won't be able to fly it yet, so I have time to build the best space ship ever. You keep it safe, Grandma!"

Mum promised she would, so with a final flurry of kisses and cuddles, Tacey managed to hustle Rory out the door and into the car.

SEVEN

If you'd only help me…

It came as a whisper on the wind, but Wystan heard it from his vantage point on the roof. He could almost feel her frustration, as if it were his own. But it was a command he could not ignore, so he slipped through the walls to where he could find her, and help.

Only to find himself at the pointy end of a sword that was almost as big as the one who wielded it.

"I can bring you in warm or I can bring you in cold, monster!" the pint sized girl proclaimed, baring her teeth.

How someone so small could wield such a large sword…

Wystan touched a finger to the underside of the blade. It was warmer than metal. More like silver gilded wood, but wood so light that…

The girl lifted the sword and thwacked it down on his hand with enough force for the blow to actually sting. A little, at least.

"That's nothing compared to what my mum will do to you if she sees you in here! No monsters allowed in the house!" she snapped.

Wystan cocked his head. "If you do not wish for my help, why did you summon me?"

Her eyes widened. "You're here to help me?"

"You asked for my help, so I came. I am bound to protect…" The red-haired woman, he almost said, for that's what the others had told him, and he knew it to be true. Yet he'd heard the child's call and answered it as a command. "It is my duty," he finished instead.

Now her eyes narrowed. "So you're not a monster, then?"

He gestured toward his wings. "I am as you see me." In monstrous form with wings and horns and a tail, just like the others.

The girl chewed her lip. "Mummy says monsters come in all shapes and forms. The worst ones look like normal people, so you don't think they're monsters until they try to hurt you. And some people look scary, but they're actually really nice. Protecting people is nice, isn't it?" Now she didn't seem so sure of herself, she lowered her sword.

"You should not lower your weapon, unless you are certain your opponent will not harm you," Wystan said, tugging the blade up to point at him again. Yes, it was light, and not particularly sharp. At worst, if wielded strongly enough, it might bruise. "But I will neither hurt you, nor allow anyone to harm you. That is the duty of a protector."

The girl nodded slowly. "Which is why you're allowed in the house. You're a nice monster protector."

He could not argue with that. "I am."

Someone hammered on the door. "Rory? Are you ready for bed yet?"

Panic flared in the girl's eyes, and she almost dropped her sword. "I'm just finishing my sword practice, Mummy!"

"Enough practice for tonight. You have one minute to get your nightie on, or it's lights out!" Mummy called through the door.

"Yes, Mummy!" Then the girl dropped her voice to a whisper. "You need to go right now, before Mummy comes. If she sees you, she'll call Auntie Callie and Auntie Octavia and they won't care if you're a good monster or a bad monster, they'll kick you right out of the house. Quick, hide!" She shoved him toward the wardrobe.

Wystan allowed her to push him inside the wardrobe. She grabbed the door and started to close it, before she changed her mind and held out the sword. "Here. So you can fight the bad monsters, if they come."

He accepted her offering in the spirit it was given, not wishing to tell her that a blow from his living stone fist would do far more damage than her flimsy weapon.

"Time's up!"

The door slammed open as darkness engulfed Wystan once more.

EIGHT

Tacey expected to find Rory still in her day clothes, but wonder of wonders, she was actually wearing her baby Yoda nightie. Even more miraculous was that she wasn't holding the plastic sword Octavia had bought her.

"Where's your sword?" Tacey asked, turning down the bed.

"In the cupboard." Rory chewed her lip, eyeing the cupboard door. Then, in a rush, she continued, "There's a monster in there and he said he's here to protect us, but…" Her bottom lip quivered, like she wanted to cry but she was trying desperately not to.

Tacey held up a hand. "What's the rule about monsters?"

Rory drew herself up. "No monsters allowed in the house!"

"Are they allowed in the cupboard?"

"No!"

If Rory's monster really did exist, Tacey felt really sorry for it right about now.

"So what do we say to monsters who dare to trespass in our house?" Tacey asked.

Rory flashed a feral grin. "On three, Mummy?" At Tacey's nod, she began to count: "One, two, THREE!"

"Get out of this house, monster, you're not welcome here. Or we'll kick you out so hard, you'll be tasting socks for a week!" they shouted together.

Rory giggled. "I still liked it better when we said we'd kick him in the bottom."

Yeah, so did Tacey, until Rory's teacher had complained about her threatening one of the little shits in her class with a well-deserved arse-kicking for stealing her stuff. So, socks it was.

"Shall we check to see if he's gone?" Tacey asked, reaching for the door handle.

Usually, Rory was really eager for this part, but now she seemed reluctant. "Will you really kick his bottom, Mummy? This one's a nice monster, even if he doesn't look very nice…"

First she wanted a demon protector, and now Rory was imagining one. This had to stop.

Tacey yanked open the cupboard door.

NINE

Wystan regarded the red-haired mother from within the walls. He only had to reach out and he'd be able to touch her puzzled face as she scanned her daughter's clothing for signs of the monster her daughter had told her about.

The monster she'd ordered out of her house. An order Wystan itched to obey, no matter how much he wanted to stay.

Then the woman picked up the sword from

the floor of the wardrobe and brandished it with as much determination as her daughter. "And if I ever see you back here again, monster, it won't just be my foot that makes contact with your arse!"

The little girl...Rory? A strange name for a girl, but he'd definitely heard her mother call her that. Rory dissolved into giggles on the bed, and her mother flashed a small smile before setting the sword down and closing the cupboard door.

The mother put her daughter to bed, and he headed up to the roof, obeying the compulsion screaming through his head. It wasn't until he reached the roof that he allowed himself to relax. It was the mother who'd summoned him in the cemetery, he was certain of it, but whatever magic had ensorcelled him made him answer the daughter's commands, too.

If his own daughter had lived...would she have been as fearless or as captivating as Rory? He would have liked it if she was.

Whereas Rory's mother was raging fire

compared to Effie's gentleness. Effie probably would have set out a saucer of milk for the monster. She certainly wouldn't have threatened him with an arse-kicking.

He smothered a laugh. He'd like to see Rory's mother try, though.

Ah, but he could never allow it, for if she did manage to kick any part of his anatomy, she'd likely hurt her foot. Living stone was far harder than human flesh. And he was bound to protect her and her daughter.

So he would stay up here on the roof, obedient to her wishes, and venture into the walls of one of the outbuildings during the day. Should she or Rory need his help, they could call and he would answer.

He would remain near enough to keep watch over her. This was a house of women, with no men to protect them until he and his kind had been summoned. Is that why they'd been summoned? Because the women needed protectors? Did danger lurk here, unseen?

He'd seen nothing so far that would make

him think so, but perhaps time would tell. He would not have believed he'd lose Effie to something as ordinary as birthing their first child.

And now here he was, bound to protect a mother and child, when he'd failed to protect his own family. Fate had given him a second chance, and he would not fail this time. Whatever the future held for Rory and her mother, he would keep them safe. After all, Rory and her mother had already survived the girl's birth. Any other danger, he could handle.

Even if he did have to watch them from the roof and the outbuildings.

It wasn't like he needed a roof over his head any more. He was made of living stone, after all.

As if to test his resolve, the clouds above him decided it was time to rain.

Wystan raised his eyes heavenward. He was a gargoyle. People had set gargoyles on their buildings to protect them from the rain for centuries. He would endure.

Then it began to hail, and Wystan let out a stream of curses unfit for any woman's ears.

43

TEN

"Good night, Rory," Tacey said as she clicked her daughter's bedroom door closed.

"G'night, Mummy," Rory mumbled from the other side.

Tacey immediately felt guilty. She probably shouldn't have let her stay up so late, watching TV with Octavia, but she liked the series so much, and it was the only time she'd had to even see Octavia, what with her working up at that mine site for weeks. Even Octavia hadn't wanted to take the contract, but when Mum had told her not to, because it was too dangerous, that'd been enough to change her mind. Not because the work was dangerous, but because Mum had said not to do it.

So when Rory wanted to spend time with her Auntie Octavia…no. Tacey hadn't been able to refuse. Even if she did have school tomorrow. But then there'd been the cricket in the bathroom basin, so Rory wouldn't brush her teeth until it was gone, and catching crickets was way harder than it looked. A pity the cat hadn't been around to deal with it. And then Rory had laughed so hard she'd accidentally spat toothpaste down the front of her baby Yoda nightie, and the only clean replacement had been the Moana one she'd gotten for Christmas, which she'd liked fine at the time, but now she screamed blue murder at being made to wear it because Moana was a princess, and Tacey had told her she wasn't, and…

Tacey leaned against the wall, wishing she could just slide down the floor and fall asleep right there on the rug. If she did, she'd probably wake up to find Callie's gargoyle statue looming over her, giving her a good view of the underside of his dangly bits.

Except it looked like Callie had hidden the statue. In her room, most likely, unless she'd taken it with her to the wedding. As long as it wasn't showing off its naked masculine glory where Rory could see it, wherever Callie had put it was fine by her.

Ah, but she couldn't sleep yet. She still had to do the grocery run, and the shops were only open for another hour. She'd written a list of all the things they needed in between cooking dinner, and Octavia had said she'd add what she needed to the list while Tacey was putting Rory to bed, but Octavia hadn't written a thing.

"Octavia! Last chance to add stuff to the shopping list, because I'm headed out!" Tacey called, trying to keep her voice down.

No answer.

And no sign of Octavia in any of the main rooms of the house, or her bedroom, either.

"Octavia!"

Still no answer.

Swearing under her breath, so that Rory wouldn't hear her, Tacey reached for her phone to put it in her bag. Only to be greeted by a swarm of blinking message and missed call icons.

Shit. She scrolled through the messages, most of which were alerts about voicemails. What was wrong with people? Couldn't they send a simple text message, instead of making her listen to them drone on?

By the time she'd listened to all the messages, she was ready to strangle Octavia. She needed her here, at home, to stay with Rory, like she'd promised, while Tacey went out.

She was probably doing yoga in the garden again. Or stargazing. Or something that occupied all her attention so she didn't even hear her sister calling her name.

It was times like these, Tacey wished she wasn't a single parent. That she had a partner, someone she could count on when she needed HELP…

For a moment, she closed her eyes and wished, sending out a plea to the universe that there was someone out there like one of the heroes in Callie's romance books, a hero who would both take care of her and support her while she pursued her dreams.

Just one man, among millions.

Who she'd probably never meet, or not even recognise if she did meet him, because there were more men like Matt in the world than perfect heroes.

And yet…she could see lights on the winding driveway. A car headed up toward Bell House.

Had the perfect romance hero taken a wrong turn that would turn out to be right?

Tacey held her breath, as the car came into view.

Damn Octavia and her tiny hatchback.

"Where have you been?" Tacey demanded, marching up to the car before Octavia had even brought it to a halt. "You said you'd stay here and watch Rory tonight, and I need to…"

"Oh, I was at the café. The manager of the backpackers called to say there'd been a break in and the police were there, and you were busy putting Rory to bed, so I answered the phone and went over to see what the damage was. It looks like they climbed through the upstairs window, then went straight for the cash register, and when they saw it was empty, they smashed one of the cake cabinets on the counter, and then left. By the time I got there, the police forensics guy was already dusting for finger prints, but he said he didn't expect to find any except ones from your staff, because there were only glove smudges on the window upstairs, so your burglar was probably wearing gloves." Octavia closed the car door and locked it behind her. "Don't worry, though. I swept up the glass, and someone will be in to repair the window first thing tomorrow morning." She glanced at her watch. "Don't you need to do the grocery shopping? The shops close in less than an hour, and you know how Callie gets if she doesn't have breakfast."

Tacey couldn't seem to close her mouth. Fuck, Octavia was the best sister in the world. Tacey threw her arms around her and hugged her hard. "You are the best, you know that? I don't know how I'd cope without you."

Octavia endured the embrace, then gently pried Tacey off her. "You wouldn't, and we both know it. Oh, and I know you said I should put what I want on the list, but…honestly, all I want is some of your cooking, to wash the taste of all that camp food out of my memory. Even your worst experimental cooking failure will taste better than THAT."

"Nothing's as bad as chili chocolate burritos," Tacey said, her tongue still burning at the memory.

"I liked those. Sure, they might have been

better with a little less spice, but Callie made more than enough margaritas to put the fire out. I think it's time for a second try. Maybe if you make a Rory-safe version, it'll taste so good, you'll be serving it for lunch in your café before you know it. I mean, who's going to say no to having chocolate for lunch?"

Any sensible mother who had a daughter like Rory, Tacey thought but didn't say. "All right, I'll race up to the shop. Rory's in bed and she should be asleep, but if she gets up…"

Octavia waved her hand. "Yeah, yeah, I know. Drink of water, trip to the toilet, whatever, just straight back to bed and no more TV until tomorrow. For her or me. I wanted to brainstorm some of the new ideas for the VR project I intend to work on tomorrow. You don't mind me working upstairs this week, do you? Rochelle's moved all her stuff out, so it's not like I'll be in her way."

Tacey nodded automatically. She didn't understand why Octavia's VR project was so important to her, but if the space above the café was her price for all her help with Rory and the café, Tacey couldn't refuse.

"Off you go and get your grocery on, then!" Octavia said, shooing Tacey toward her own car.

Sometimes Tacey wondered which one of them was supposed to be the older, more organised sister. But right now, she didn't care.

ELEVEN

This time, Wystan doesn't so much as hear the call as feel it in his bones, dragging him down from the roof and into the garden. Only he forced himself to stop in the shadow on the veranda, to take a breath to steel himself before he presented himself to her. He couldn't afford to mess this up, or she'd banish him to the roof again. To protect her, she needed to allow him to stay close, with no walls between them.

Which meant he had to make a good enough impression to make her reconsider her no monsters in the house rule. Or at least to allow him to be an exception to that rule…

This would take some real fancy talking, which wasn't exactly his strength. All his life he'd been a farmer, and farmers were anything but fancy. Damn, he wished Effie were here to help him now.

Powerful bright lights blinded him, moving up the drive. It was one of those horseless carriages these girls all seemed to possess, with the red haired woman's sister at the wheel. Tacey, her name was, he'd learned, though he suspected it was a pet name for something else. After all, the sister's name was Octavia, so Tacey's parents had surely bestowed her with a similarly formal, Latin-sounding name.

Then again, she called her daughter Rory…

The two women talked of a burglary at a café. The place Tacey worked, he surmised, if that was where she went early each morning, before anyone else in the house was awake.

Perhaps that was where she needed protecting, instead of this house she shared with her daughter and her sister. Oh, and the witch, who'd disappeared with Grant. If he'd expected trouble from anyone, it would have been those two, but with them gone, this house was so calm, he couldn't understand why Tacey needed a protector.

So after Tacey returned from her shopping trip, and she and her sister retired for the night, he watched and waited for…well, something to happen, and when it did not, he firmed up his resolve. When Tacey left for work in the morning, he would go with her to the café, and watch over her there.

The moon was still high in the sky, with no sign of the coming dawn, when Tacey set off in her horseless carriage the next day. She did not seem to notice the flying shape high above her, not even when she stopped at a red light that evidently signalled some sort of warning Wystan did not understand.

Finally, she drew her carriage up in front of the glass fronted windows of the Shut Up Café. Wystan could only stare. He couldn't imagine anyone in his time allowing such a coarsely named café to exist, let alone proclaim its name to all and sundry in a well-lit sign facing the street, yet here it was.

The interior was dark as she turned the key in the lock and opened the doors, slipping quickly inside before slamming them shut behind her, as though she did not want him to follow.

Wystan did not mind. In fact, he'd expected to have to keep his distance, so he'd already taken up a vantage point on top of the building across the road from the café, beside a squat gargoyle statue with an unspeakably smug expression. Wystan was tempted to tip it off the roof to smash on the road below, but he stayed his hand. Better not to alert anyone to his watchful presence.

When the sky began to lighten, he crossed the street and slid between the walls of the café, so that he might continue to keep watch over her during daylight.

He watched, all right…and he couldn't seem to drag his eyes away from her. Tacey was not a mere employee, but the proprietress of the café, which served everyone from common workers in dust-stained clothes up to fancy men in formal suits. Stranger still, she served them all the same, making everyone line up for service as though every man or woman who came into her establishment was equal. And the way she served them…it was like she was at home, and they were her guests, not her customers. For the first time, he was reminded of Effie, though Tacey looked nothing like her. All hard lines to Effie's softness, and tall as a man, where Effie had barely come up to his shoulder.

Oh, and Tacey could cook…the delectable scents that wafted out of her kitchen were enough to make even a gargoyle drool. Thank the heavens he was within the walls when he did, or he would have left a mighty puddle by the end of the day. Muffins, cakes, biscuits and all manner of savoury things, in addition to cup after cup of coffee that smelled better than any brew he'd ever drunk.

A thousand times, he found himself wanting to venture out from his hiding place. To introduce himself to her as her protector. To ask for a cup of coffee, even if only to inhale the scent, for he had no need to drink it. Or walk up to the counter, look her in the eye and beg her to reconsider her rule about monsters, for surely the café owner who treated every man the same, whether high class or low, could find it in her heart to be civil to someone like him…

But he resisted, and remained within the walls, until finally the sun set and he stationed himself on a neighbouring rooftop again, for with distance, it was slightly easier to resist temptation. Not to mention that up here, he was reminded that the smug, squat gargoyle watched his every move, judging.

When night fell, he followed her carriage to

Rory's school, where she collected the girl before heading back home to the house she shared with her sister. Completely unaware of the protector who followed and watched over her.

His days and nights fell into a pattern, following Tacey to work and home again, watching over her at night before heading to the café with her before dawn. It was a comfortable existence, being Tacey's protector, for there was very little actual protecting to do. All he did was stand watch, and wait.

Until one morning…he learned why he'd been summoned.

TWELVE

Tacey wasn't sure what was wrong with her this week. She jumped at the smallest sound, and she could have sworn she felt someone was watching her at least a dozen times a day, but when she looked around, she couldn't see anyone paying her particular attention. Still, she didn't let it dim the pride she took in her work, whether it was cooking, brewing, serving or doing the books, which she'd put off until

Saturday morning, but she knew she couldn't wait any longer.

Besides, she needed to know where she stood financially. The pandemic had closed her café for weeks, and even with government assistance, they'd barely managed to keep afloat until they'd been allowed to reopen again. It hadn't helped that it was still hard to get the most basic supplies. What had possessed people stuck at home to want to bake their own bread? The shortage of flour and yeast didn't concern them now they were all back at work and school, but every bakery and café was fighting to get enough, and the suppliers were hiking the prices, for no other reason than to increase their own profit margin at the expense of already battling business owners.

Ooh, if she'd been in charge of emergency measures instead of that dipshit of a prime minister…

Tacey shook her head. She ran a café, not a country, and even that was a struggle some days. Especially today, when she had to work and take care of Rory. Luckily, Rory was happily ensconced upstairs with some art supplies, a selection of muffins and a hot chocolate, so she'd have time to finish the month's financials before Rory needed anything else.

She added everything up, and then checked it all over again, just to be sure. Only then did she sit back and allow herself to smile.

Finally, the café was back on track. They'd reopened only a few weeks ago, with low expectations and no idea how well they'd go, but if these numbers were correct – and they should be, she'd checked them twice – this last week had actually been more profitable than the weeks before the pandemic started. If she could keep this up, or maybe even grow the business, she'd have a house deposit by year's end. Maybe even one big enough to afford a place with a backyard that wasn't snake infested bush like Bell House, where Rory could actually have a lawn and play outside.

Or, better yet, a park nearby with lawn that the council took care of, so Rory could still have the lawn and Tacey wouldn't have to mow it.

She could dream, couldn't she?

But she'd need more than one profitable month to make it happen. This month and next month and the one after that, all the way into next year, or whenever she actually applied for a mortgage. Then she still had to keep the café going so she could afford the mortgage repayments…

Which meant good business planning, based on this month's data, for next month.

Rostering, ordering, forecasting, menu planning…

Tacey wasn't sure if it was hours or merely minutes later when she heard someone ringing the bell on the counter for service. Which was weird, because Rochelle was out there this morning, and Rochelle was one of her best staff. Better than Octavia, even, because Rochelle was a master at latte art, and if there was one thing Tacey's customers liked better than a well-brewed coffee, it was a pretty, well-brewed coffee. If she could only persuade Ben to put some of his artwork on the milk froth as well as on paper…

Rochelle appeared in the office doorway, looking distinctly pissed off, an expression Tacey couldn't ever remember seeing on her face before. "I'm sorry to interrupt you while you're doing month end, but there's a customer at the counter who insists on talking to the manager."

Tacey rose, pasting her take-no-shit smile on her face. "Is her name Karen?" Because Tacey was ready to refund the bitch's entire order and shove her out the door, never to return.

Rochelle swallowed, glancing nervously over her shoulder. "No, I don't think so. I wish Ben was here."

Now alarm bells were ringing in Tacey's head, louder than the actual bell on the counter.

"You stay here, and I'll go see to this

customer. When I have their attention, you sneak out and head for the police station. Tell them…tell them anyone who's working in the police station this morning can have a free coffee and a muffin if they come down to the café before noon." Just in case. Not that they'd ever had a customer so abusive they'd needed to call the police, and Tacey was ninety percent certain she'd send this one on their way without a problem, but still…

Rochelle bobbed her head frantically.

Tacey blew out a threat and marched out to deal with whatever trouble had come to her café.

THIRTEEN

The moment Tacey stepped into the café, she knew this was no Karen. Unless Karens were now built like brick shithouses and stole their suits from the Rock. She edged behind the counter, wanting something solid between her and whoever this dick was before she spoke to him.

"I'm the manager here. How can I help you, sir?" she said as she raised her eyes to his face.

And froze.

"You're going to hand over my daughter, bitch, because she belongs to me," Matt hissed, with a malevolent stare the like of which she'd never seen on his usually charming face.

Prison had changed him. Not just the muscles, but inside his head, too.

"You want…what?" Tacey could barely get the words out.

"My daughter. You stole her from me, along with five years of my life, and I want them back."

Nope. No words. Matt had gone mad.

In the corner of her eye, she saw Rochelle dash out the door, and down the street, toward the police station. Tacey crossed her fingers they really wanted free coffee right now.

Matt leaned on the counter, towering over her like he was used to intimidating people. "I'll tell you how this is going to go. In two weeks' time, on a Saturday morning, I'm going to come back here to pick up my daughter. If you have any sense, or if you ever want to see her again, you'll come with us."

When hell froze over. Tacey opened her mouth to say so.

Matt held up a finger. "Now if you're stupid, or maybe just stubborn, we'll take this through the courts, and I'll tell the judge all about your paranoid delusions that got me locked up, and I'll also tell them about the fake PR you've been getting for your café with the guy in the suit. In fact, how about I tell the police about him, and have you charged for fraud. Then you'll go to prison, and you'll never see your daughter again. I'll make sure of it."

Court and delusions and…fraud? "Do you mean the Moth Man videos?" Tacey blurted out. "Because I didn't take those. I wasn't even here. Someone else took them through the café window and put them on the internet. All I did was offer free coffee to anyone who could film the creature again, and no one ever did, so…" She shrugged.

"Don't play stupid with me. I saw the guy in the suit right here inside, talking to you. I've got it all on film."

Now who was being delusional? Tacey had never talked to anyone dressed like the Moth Man.

"Two weeks. Saturday morning. Right here. And if she's not here, you'll wish you'd died in that car, years ago." He turned on his heel and stalked out.

It wasn't until the door had closed behind him that Tacey dared to breathe again.

FOURTEEN

Help. There's a monster here. A bad one.

The call summoned Wystan not to the café, but to the floor above, where he found Rory huddled beneath the couch. The only problem was…sunlight streamed through the windows into the room, trapping him within the walls.

He moved to the wall closest to her hiding place and said, "I'm here, Rory. Here to protect you. But I can't come out until it's dark. Sunlight hurts me. Can you close the curtains?"

"They're blinds, Mr Monster," Rory whispered.

"Those, then."

A long pause. "Maybe."

But she did crawl out from under the couch and head for the nearest window.

It took her a while, but she managed to close enough of them for the room to become surprisingly dark. Wystan stuck his hand out of the wall. When his fingers didn't turn to stone, he stepped out completely.

"Will you protect me from the monster?" Rory asked.

"Of course I will," Wystan said. "Where is it?"

Rory pointed at the floor. "Downstairs in the café. He was rude to Rochelle, and then he asked to see the manager. That's Mummy. But he's a monster. I know he is."

Curious, Wystan edged toward the stairs, so he might get a better look. He couldn't see much more than a man's broad back, clad in fine wool suit cloth, but he could hear just fine.

"How can I help you, sir?" Tacey asked, in her excessively polite but hard as nails tone that made the words sound surprisingly more like FUCK OFF. Words he'd never actually heard her say to a customer, but when the café was empty, in the privacy of the kitchen…

Wystan's mouth dropped open. The man Rory called a monster was claiming to be the girl's father, and demanding his rights as such.

Wystan's heart constricted in his chest at the thought of not being able to see his own child for five years. Of Effie stealing the baby away so he never saw her…it was almost as bad as losing them forever, knowing they were somewhere, but he couldn't see them…

Not to mention the man was wealthy, to be wearing such a fine suit. Wouldn't the child be better off with her father, who could provide her with every luxury? Wouldn't Tacey be better off with him, too, instead of working for a living like she did now?

The door closed downstairs, and the man was gone. A long moment passed, before the next sound he heard was feet thundering up the stairs.

"Rory, are you up here?" Tacey called.

Rory threw herself at Wystan's feet and wrapped her arms tightly around his legs. "You can't let the monster take me!"

And Tacey flicked on the light.

FIFTEEN

Tacey blinked. First, she wondered how Callie had managed to get her naked gargoyle statue up here. Second, she wondered why. Then she took in the image of her daughter hugging the statue's ankles and wondered if she could get the girl out of there before she looked up and saw the gargoyle's massive package.

If anything, it was even bigger than she remembered.

"Come on, Rory, it's time to go home," Tacey said, holding out her hand to help her up.

Rory only wrapped her arms tighter around the statue's ankles. "Not without Mr Monster Protector. He's here to protect me!"

Tacey sighed. Of course Rory would take a liking to the naked statue. When Callie got back, Tacey was going to kick her arse into next week.

"I can't carry him down the stairs, sweetheart. We'll have to come back for him later, when we can find someone strong enough to help move him." Move him to somewhere Rory wouldn't find him.

"Don't be silly. He can walk, Mummy!"

Tacey took a deep breath. "Rory, statues can't…"

"And he can talk, too! He's a not a statue, he's a…" Rory squinted up at the statue. "Mr Monster, what kind of monster are you?"

One more second and she was going to see his package and start asking other questions

Tacey wasn't sure she wanted to answer yet.

"I'm a gargoyle, Miss Rory, and my name is Wystan Steel."

It moved. The statue actually moved. Or maybe Matt was right and she was delusional, and…

Tacey swore.

"Language, Mummy!"

Fuck.

The man in the suit. He was just a man in a suit. Matt must have seen Rochelle or Octavia talking to him, and thought…

Well, that explained the impressive package. It had to be fake, too. Made of the same rubbery plastic as Callie's statue.

Tacey reached out to give it a squeeze.

It didn't feel like rubber at all. It was warm and hard and soft all at the same time, like steel wrapped in silk. Like a man's actual…

Tacey swore again and released the man's…member. She'd never seen a dick that big before. How could she possibly have thought it was real?

She bit her lip, trying and failing to meet the man's eyes. Of course, he was covered in makeup and costume and he looked like a statue, but she still knew he was a man under all that and she'd just grabbed his dick and given it a good squeeze. "Sorry." It came out like the squeak of a dying mouse.

His mouth opened, then closed again, without any words coming out. The man marched up to the wall and just sort of…disappeared.

Leaving Tacey and Rory staring after him.

Rory, of course, recovered first. "You scared him away, Mummy! He promised to protect me!" she wailed.

"I'll protect you, sweetheart. That's what mummies do," Tacey said absently. She didn't know how she'd do it yet, but she knew she'd do anything to protect Rory from Matt. He wasn't having her, not while Tacey still drew breath. She'd fight him every step of the way.

As for whatever she'd just seen…she intended to do her best to forget it, and make sure Rory did, too. She had enough to deal with, just with Matt.

SIXTEEN

When they got home, Rory insisted she wanted to watch TV, and Tacey was too distracted to say no. Her mind was full of dread and possible solutions, each crazier than the last. Moving somewhere else was out of the question, what with the borders closed and all her family and friends were here. Besides, even if she did go somewhere else, Matt had the money to hire someone to hunt her down.

She wished she'd had surveillance cameras in the café, to capture that conversation to prove to the police that the first thing Matt did when he got out of prison was to find her and threaten her life. Definitely not the actions of an innocent man.

She could try to get a restraining order, she supposed, but he'd only appeal it in court, and if he had a lawyer who'd managed to get his entire conviction overturned, the restraining order wouldn't be worth the paper it was printed on.

She couldn't surrender Rory to him, but maybe if she went with her, to make sure she was okay…

No. Just NO.

In the end, Tacey tried to clean the house to settle her spiralling mind, but it didn't help. By the time she put Rory to bed that night, the house was sparkling clean, and her body was exhausted, but her mind was still spinning like a jet engine.

Worse, it was just her and Rory tonight.

Callie was still down south, Alethea was still housesitting for her parents, Sybil was somewhere in the Arctic Circle on the archaeological dig of a lifetime, and Octavia was working.

So with no one else to talk to, a big glass of wine was probably the only way she was going to get her mind to settle enough to sleep tonight. Well, wine or something stronger…

Yeah, definitely something stronger. The rest of that bottle of vodka they'd taken to the cemetery that night they'd tried and failed to summon a demon should do it.

First the Moth Man, then a demon, and today, a gargoyle with a monster cock. Well, a man dressed like one, anyway.

What had he said his name was? It was weird, that was for sure. Winston…no, Wystan Steel, that was it.

Octavia or Rochelle had probably hired him to do some more PR videos for the café. Tacey couldn't remember agreeing to pay for that, but maybe he'd done it as a favour for them.

After all, Octavia took all sorts of payment when she fixed people's computers, and Rochelle did some work as a paid actor at Fremantle Prison.

Why they'd picked a man with a monster cock to play a monster, though…

Tacey couldn't help but think about what it had looked and felt like. If she closed her eyes, she saw that perfect package again, looking like the bits of a grey stone statue, but hot and hard and probably amazing inside you once you got naked with him.

Tacey shook herself. She couldn't remember the last time she'd slept with a man. Definitely before Rory was born. Hell, it might even have been Matt. And it'd probably be years more before she dared to date again. She should probably just bite the bullet and go buy a vibrator, like the girls in Callie's romance books did. All the American women seemed to own one, while she didn't know a single Aussie girl who did. Sex shops here sold them, though, so someone must be buying them.

She'd have to actually go into the shop to get one, though, instead of ordering one online, because if one of the other girls saw the package and opened it…she'd never live it down.

Now she really needed that vodka.

Tacey opened her eyes, blinked, then closed them again.

She was not delusional. When she opened her eyes again, she'd discover she'd just imagined seeing that monster cock in her lounge room, and she'd only seen it in her mind's eye. Wystan Steel's dick and all the rest of him could not possibly be standing in front of her, in her house.

She opened her eyes.

"You have until the count of three to get out of my fucking house, or I'm calling the police. And I'm going to spend every second you're still trespassing on my property kicking your arse!" She reached for the nearest object she could use as a weapon, which turned out to be Rory's plastic sword, and brandished it.

"Get out!"

Wystan backed away with his hands up, but he didn't go far. "Mistress Tacey, as I tried to tell Miss Rory, you can't hurt me with that. I'm your gargoyle protector, and I'm made of living stone, the better to defend you. Even if that were a real sword, it could not pierce my skin."

Tacey dropped the sword on the floor in disgust. She wouldn't have allowed Rory to have a sword at all unless she'd been sure she couldn't hurt herself with it.

"How did you get in here?" she demanded.

"Gargoyles have the uncanny talent of being able to walk through walls."

She opened her mouth to tell him he wasn't a gargoyle and no one could walk through walls, but that image of him disappearing in the studio above the café…he'd just put his back to the wall and…poof, gone.

"But why are you here?" she persisted. Because none of today made any sense. First Matt, now Wystan…

"You summoned me. You and your friends in the cemetery."

"You're a demon?" she squeaked, leaping onto the couch. Like he was a cockroach skittering across the floor that she could avoid if she got up high enough.

He sighed. "I'm a gargoyle, Miss Tacey."

She considered telling him to call her Miss Bell, but she hated being called that. "Just Tacey. And you're…Wystan?"

He nodded once.

"Your gargoyle protector, and Miss Rory's, too. I told her this some days ago, but the timing never seemed right to introduce myself to you until today."

Some days ago…like the night after the summoning when Rory had come home from visiting Mum? "The imaginary monster in her cupboard, the one she gave her sword to because she said it was a good monster…that was YOU?"

"Yes."

"And you promised to protect her?"

Another nod.

Tacey's shoulders slumped in relief. "So you're here to stop Matt from taking her. To protect her from him."

"Is Matt the man who came to the café today? The one claiming to be her father?"

"He is her father." It might not be written on her birth certificate, but Tacey knew it was true.

The gargoyle looked troubled. "I am sworn to protect her from harm, but I cannot, in good conscience, keep a child away from her rightful father. Or a wife from her husband. Perhaps if you merely went to him and apologised for running away from him with his child, he would forgive you and you could be a family again." His eyes turned wistful. Like he wished his family would do that, whoever and wherever they were.

Huh. Gargoyle families. She guessed they had to exist. Well, if gargoyles existed, then little gargoyles had to come from somewhere, and…

"Why do you not simply ask for his forgiveness?"

Tacey coughed out a laugh. "You think I should beg Matt to forgive me for him trying to kill us before Rory was born? Uh, no. I didn't run. He's the one who went to prison for trying to kill us. I just tried to get on with my life, and bringing up Rory. Until he got out of prison this week, because some fancy lawyer and likely a corrupt judge got together and released him."

Wystan's eyes widened. "He tried to kill you? How did you manage to survive?"

Well, that was a fair question. Even before he went to prison, Matt had been a big guy. And strong, like all swimmers. Nothing like the muscles he'd bulked on since, but still…

"Well, I suppose I survived because I both loved and hated his car…" she began.

Wystan only looked confused.

"You know my car, the one I drive to work in?" she asked.

He nodded.

"Well, he had an old classic Holden. Big and beautiful, but no safety features to speak of, not like mine. So when it's in a crash, no airbags come out to cushion you so you don't get hurt. Anyway, he took my car to work one day, making some excuse about how he didn't want to park his outside with the bad weather forecast, because he'd just had one of the panels repainted. So when I needed to go to the shop to get something, I had to borrow his car. What I didn't know was that he'd cut the brakes…the things that make the car slow down or stop…so when you pressed them, instead of stopping, the car just kept on going until it crashed. Only I was really nervous driving it, so I reversed out onto the lawn instead of the street, and when I tried to stop reversing so I could go forward, it wouldn't stop, until the back bumped into the fence and broke the lights. I was too scared to drive it at that point, so I called a tow truck to take it to the mechanic to get the lights fixed before Matt came home and saw what I'd done, only the mechanic saw the damage to the brakes, which he'd replaced only a few months beforehand, and reported it to the police.

"At first, they started investigating people who might want to kill Matt, because they thought he was the target. Then they started talking to the neighbours, and a few of them had seen him working on the car. Then one of them accidentally opened a letter they thought was for them, but it turned out to have been addressed to me, with a life insurance policy Matt had taken out on me…and suddenly I was the target, and Matt was their main suspect…"

Wystan looked horrified. "Your husband tried to kill you?"

Tacey laughed shakily. "Oh, he's not my husband. We were engaged, because his family was Catholic and he didn't want Rory to be born out of wedlock or whatever, but then they died in a car crash…like Matt, his dad also drove a classic car with no safety features, and they hit a kangaroo that came out of nowhere, so his parents just had no chance…so we agreed to postpone the wedding until after Rory was born. Anyway, Matt was their only child, so he inherited everything, including their superannuation and life insurance, so he went from struggling to work and study and save for a deposit to buy a cheap house for us, to owning his parents' riverfront mansion and never having to work again. He insisted I move in with him there, so I did, but then he got kind of distant. I figured it was just grief over losing his parents, but it turned out he was plotting to kill me so he could have more money from my life insurance." She had a sudden, terrible thought. "You know, he probably still has that policy, too. I mean, as long as he still had the money to pay it…if anything happened to me, he'd be even richer. If he's taken out a policy on Rory, too…that's why I can't let him have her. I can't trust him. The bastard tried to kill us, and a whole jury convicted him of the crime, so whatever that corrupt judge says, I won't believe he's innocent. I can't."

Wystan nodded gravely. "I'm sworn to protect both you and Miss Rory. If this man is a danger to you, then that is what I shall do. I will watch over you both at night, but…during the day, when you are at work and she goes to school, what would you have me do?"

Well, there was one bright spot, at least. "Today's the first day of the school holidays, so she can come to work with me. That way, you could watch over both of us in the café during the day." She frowned. "Though you'll need some clothes on if you're going to be out in public. You can't just let everything hang out like that. At the very least, you'll need pants." She felt her face redden as she did her best not to look down.

"I assure you, no one will see me unless I wish them to. I have grown quite skilled at hiding, even in your café. But clothing seems like a sensible idea, in case I do need to show myself. Where might I find something suitable?"

Tacey thought for a moment. "Well, I don't think anything of mine will fit you, and the other girls wear…well, ladies' clothes, most of the time. There might be some men's clothes up in the attic, though, from people who've lived here before us. You could take anything you like from up there."

"I shall watch over you as you sleep tonight, and in the morning, I shall be ready and properly attired, as you wish."

As you wish. Those three words did things to her insides that she'd thought only happened in romance books. Or the Princess Bride, of course.

"Don't make me regret this," she warned him.

SEVENTEEN

When Tacey led a yawning Rory out to the car in the pre-dawn darkness, he was already waiting for her. For a moment, she thought he'd forgotten about the pants, until she realised he hadn't, but…

"Where on Earth did you find those?"

Wystan glanced down. "They were in the attic, just like you said. They seemed the sturdiest ones there."

Well, sure, leather was sturdy, but it also clung to every muscle and…everything else, too. She could see his cock so clearly, he might as well not be wearing any pants at all.

"And I take it gargoyles don't do shirts?" she asked, trying not to look at the muscles above the pants. This dude was definitely ripped.

He shrugged. "A shirt would foul my wings, so that I could not fly behind your carriage to the café."

A shirt would…what?

"You are absolutely not following me in the air to the café. A police chopper, lights and all, would be less noticeable. You can come in the car, or not at all."

Rory tugged her hand out of Tacey's and reached for Wystan's instead. "You can sit with me in the back seat."

Only Rory could possibly befriend a monster this fast. And when he seemed unfamiliar with seat belts, she helped him with that, too.

It was kindness and innocence like hers that predatory monsters took advantage of, not caring who they hurt or how much. Tacey closed her eyes. This was a mistake. A terrible, terrible mistake that she was going to regret…

"We are securely fastened into our seats, Tacey. We can depart," Wystan said.

Tacey blew out a breath. She couldn't say it in front of Rory, but when they got to the café, she was going to take Wystan aside and tell him in no uncertain terms that the deal was off. She'd find an ordinary way to deal with this mess, without any sort of paranormal assistance. Well-endowed or otherwise.

The drive to the café took almost no time at all. Damn non-existent early morning traffic.

Tacey unlocked the door and led the way in, flicking the lights on as she went. She glanced at the stairs, debating.

"Can I go and sit on Auntie Octavia's sofa upstairs, Mummy?" Rory asked.

Not if Octavia had been up all night on her computer and had fallen asleep up there.

"Sweetheart, Auntie Octavia might still be asleep…" Tacey began.

Wystan shook his head. "We are the only people in the building. There is no one upstairs."

Rory held out her hand. "Come on, Mr Monster. I have colouring to do before breakfast, and you can help."

Tacey frowned. "You go on up and unpack your things. I need to talk to Mr Steel for a minute first."

Rory rolled her eyes. "Ooookaaaay," she huffed as she lugged her satchel of art supplies up the stairs.

The moment Rory was out of earshot, Tacey turned to the gargoyle. "If you hurt her, or say or do anything that causes her the slightest bit of discomfort, I will boot you back out those doors so fast, you won't know what hit you."

"No harm will come to your daughter while I am her protector. I swear it," Wystan said.

She wanted to believe him. She really did. It

was just…this massive man, with the wings and…

Hadn't Matt said something about seeing her talking to a man in a Moth Man suit? Well, someone he'd thought was her, anyway. Which meant he'd been watching the café somehow. Either spying on her from outside or…

Tacey scanned the ceiling. The baleful red eye of a security camera she'd never noticed before stared at her from the corner behind the espresso machine.

"That will have to go," she muttered.

A moment later, Wystan leaped into the air, enormous wings flapping to keep him aloft, as his meaty fist smashed the camera right off the wall. Pieces of glass, plastic and electrical innards rained down on the tiles. She half expected to see sparking wiring dangling from the ceiling, but there was nothing but a dent in the plaster to show the camera had ever been up there.

She grabbed the dustpan and brush and shoved it into Wystan's hands. "You made the mess, you can clean it up. Then you can go up and keep an eye on Rory. I need to start baking."

He inclined his head. "Yes, mistress."

And then, just when she thought he couldn't get an hotter, he knelt on the floor in those tight leather pants and swept up all the camera components without a word of complaint. She'd never seen anything so sexy in her life.

"Where is your midden heap?"

Midden? Wasn't that what archaeologists dug up? She was sure she'd heard Alethea use the word once or twice. It was where…oh.

"Tip it in the bin, there," Tacey pointed.

He carefully brushed out every last bit of rubbish, then returned the dustpan and brush to their spot under the counter, before climbing the stairs to Rory.

Tacey couldn't help but watch every step he took in those tight leather pants, hugging that firm arse that looked positively lickable.

If Wystan hadn't been a monster, Tacey

could have sworn she was in love. As it was, she was more than a little in lust.

But she didn't have time to indulge that sort of passion right now. She had to save all her passion for her baking, or there wouldn't be any breakfast when the café opened, and that would never do.

EIGHTEEN

When Tacey took the last tray of muffins out of the oven and replaced it with one filled with carefully shaped cookies, the sun was almost rising. She probably had just enough time to take breakfast up to Rory and Wystan before the first batch of cookies were done, so she picked out a selection of her best muffins, added an extra chocolate one for Rory who wouldn't eat anything else, arranged them carefully in a basket with plates and serviettes, and headed upstairs.

She set the basket down on the table and eyed the blinds. Sunlight was already peeking around the edges. Time to turn the lights off, and let sunlight in. She marched over to the window, yanked the blind cord and began tying it to the cleat.

"No, Mummy, NO!" Rory screamed.

Tacey turned. "What is it? Is the muffin too hot?" She was sure she'd grabbed one of the cooled ones, but it might have still been warm in the middle…

"No! You're hurting Mr Monster!" she wailed as she tugged the quilt off Octavia's bed and tried to drag it across the floor to where Wystan was standing.

"He's fine, Rory. Aren't you, Wystan?"

No response. Wystan didn't even move. Like he was a statue or something. Or a…gargoyle…

Tacey marched up to him, then hesitated. She swallowed, then poked him in the shoulder. Hard. He didn't move at all. Hell, his hard body didn't give in the slightest, even as she pushed harder. Like he really was nothing but a stone statue.

Rory flapped the quilt at his legs. "Help me, Mummy! The sun hurts him. We need to cover him up!"

It took Tacey a moment to realise Rory was trying to toss the quilt over his head, only she couldn't reach up high enough. Tacey grabbed one edge and dragged the black, star-printed fabric over the statue.

Rory dropped to her knees on the floor and tugged the quilt down so it covered his feet. When she was satisfied, she raced over to the window and pulled down the blind.

Darkness descended on the room again. But it wasn't dark enough for Tacey to miss movement beneath the quilt.

Or Wystan's muffled voice, saying, "Thank you, Miss Rory and Mistress Tacey," before he pulled the quilt off, and bundled it into his arms.

Tacey folded her arms across her chest. "Sunlight hurts you, hmm? Don't you think you should have mentioned something like that, when you were promising to protect my daughter?" Men. Bloody useless, the lot of them. Even the winged ones.

Wystan hung his head. "It's not so much a weakness as a gargoyle thing. In direct sunlight, gargoyles turn to stone. As you saw." He coughed. "If I'd had more than a moment's warning, I might have been able to take shelter within the walls, where the light could not reach me. If Miss Rory was in danger, I could have pulled her inside the walls with me."

Rory's eyes widened. "You can walk through walls?"

"You are not dragging my daughter through walls. Not now, not ever. Do I make myself clear?" Shit, what if he tried to do it and she got stuck? Rory could die, or be horribly hurt. Tacey suppressed a shudder.

Wystan frowned. "But Mistress Tacey…"

"No walking through walls with my

daughter. Or you can walk through all the walls by yourself until you're out of my café, and never come back." Because what use was a protector who couldn't come out in daylight? She knew this had been a mistake.

"Yes, Mistress Tacey." The words came out through gritted teeth, and she half expected him to storm out, but he stayed where he was. His only movement was to turn his attention back to Rory, who'd gone back to her colouring in on the floor.

She felt almost bad for ordering him around. He had volunteered to protect Rory, after all. It wasn't like she was paying him. Yet.

Tacey waved at the basket of muffins. "I brought you breakfast. For both of you. If you need more, just sing out, and I'll bring up more from the kitchen."

Rory looked up from her colouring. "I can come and get them, Mummy. Sunlight doesn't hurt me."

Tacey wasn't sure whether to be proud of her daughter, or worried, or both. Her kindness to a monster like Wystan was remarkable, but it was also likely to lead to people taking advantage of her. Tacey sighed. "No, sweetheart. You stay upstairs with the blinds down so Wystan can protect you, okay? If you need anything, let me know and I can bring it up."

She expected Rory to argue.

But Rory just nodded. "He's protecting me from the bad monsters, isn't he, Mummy?"

Tacey swallowed. That she trusted Wystan, an actual monster, with her daughter more than she trusted the girl's own father…but no matter what the courts said, Matt had tried to kill them both. That made him a monster more monstrous than Wystan had been only a few minutes ago.

A monster she needed to find a better way to vanquish than giving her daughter a gargoyle bodyguard.

Tacey sighed. She'd deal with that issue after she'd opened the café and dealt with the morning breakfast rush. First, she had to fire up the espresso machine and placate all the caffeine addicts already queueing up outside the door.

NINETEEN

"Wow, it looks just like an angel," the girl breathed as Tacey set her coffee down.

The guy sitting across from her peered at his cup. "Mine looks more like the Moth Man. If I take a video of it with my phone, do I still get free coffee for a year?"

Tacey laughed. "Sorry, no. That offer only applies if you capture video of the real Moth Man, not just his likeness in your latte."

The guy turned to the girl. "Want to come back after the exam, and see if we can spot him?"

She pouted. "We'll see. I'd rather go to a bar than drink coffee after this one. Family law is the worst. I'd rather spend my whole life drawing up real estate contracts than try to come up with another case for sole custody. I swear, it's like when parents get divorced, they forget their kids are people, too, instead of possessions they can use for cheap point scoring over their former partner."

"It's not all bad. I mean, what if the reason one parent wants sole custody is because the other one's an abusive piece of shit? If you won a case like that, you and the parent with sole custody would be saving the kid from a horrible childhood."

"Yeah, but then you have to hear about the abuse that's already happened and I just…can't…" The girl's eyes filled with tears. "It's all horrible."

"Well, we know neither of us is going into

family law, but we still need to pass this exam, so drink up and let's get some last minute cramming done before we have to head back."

The girl nodded and Tacey headed back to the counter.

That was the answer, then. If she wanted to keep Rory safe from Matt, she'd need to take him to court, and fight him where it mattered. But to do that, she'd need the best family lawyer in Perth. That wouldn't come cheap.

She swallowed. She had her savings for a house deposit, and she had the café. There was no point buying a house for her and Rory to live in if Matt got custody of her. Better to live with Rory in Bell House for the next ten years than hand her over to him. Shit, she'd sell the café, too, if it meant she could keep Rory safe.

"Good morning, Tacey. Has it been busy today?"

Tacey looked up. Was it almost lunchtime already? Wow, yeah. And Rochelle looked…positively glowing. Almost a different person to the nervous shadow who'd begged to stay in the studio upstairs only a few weeks ago. Ditching that arsehole boyfriend and hooking up with their artist in residence had definitely helped, too, but it was more like she'd stopped allowing that vampire to suck the life out of her and let Ben breathe life into her instead.

The world would be a better place with more Bens in it. Or even just one more in her life...

Tacey sighed. "Yeah, it's been flat out. I haven't even finished making all the paninis for today. Could you take over the counter while I take care of them?"

Rochelle squinted at the sandwich cabinet. "What are we missing? Everything looks like it's here."

"All the regular items, yeah, but I had this crazy idea last week to do a Christmas in July thing during the school holidays. The gingerbread muffins are all gone, but the cookies haven't been as popular. I figured I'd try the cranberry eggnog muffins tomorrow, but I wanted to have the turkey paninis for today's lunch, only the turkey was too hot when I took it out of the oven, so I was waiting for it to be cool enough to touch before I made them up."

Now I had her interest. "What else are you putting in them?"

"Well, there's honey roasted pumpkin and baby spinach leaves. I was thinking of adding some feta, but I thought…at Christmas, you'd more likely to have a cheeseboard with brie or smoked cheese or something, wouldn't you?"

Rochelle nodded slowly. "Oh, yeah, it would be amazing with a bit of brie. Maybe with sweet chili sauce, too?"

Tacey thought about it. "Maybe. We're all out of chili sauce, but there's a delivery due tomorrow. I'll see how they sell today, and if they do well, tomorrow I'll do half spicy, half mild."

"Keep one aside for me, please. Today and tomorrow," Rochelle said.

Tacey promised to do just that, as she

headed into the kitchen. The sandwiches didn't take long, and once they were neatly stacked in the cabinet with the rest of today's lunch options, she figured she was due a break.

Of course, that's when the lunch rush started, and it was a couple of hours before she had a moment to find the name of a lawyer worth talking to, and another hour of going through all manner of reviews before she had one name: Dominic Lamont.

No time like the present, she told herself. If she waited, the mid afternoon coffee rush would start, and she wouldn't get another chance to call until tomorrow.

She dialled, and held her breath.

The receptionist answered on the second ring. "This is Lamont and Partners. How may I direct your call?"

Tacey opened her mouth, but no sound came out. She cleared her throat and tried again. "I need a lawyer for a custody case, and I want to hire Dominic Lamont."

"Mr Lamont has a full case load at the

moment, and he isn't taking any new clients, but perhaps one of our other partners…"

"It has to be him. My ex tried to kill us and now he's trying to get custody of our daughter. Please, he just got out of prison and this case will definitely get media coverage. I know Mr Lamont prefers to take high profile cases. My ex is Matthew Masters. He's been all over the news."

A pause that seemed to stretch forever. "Can I put you on hold, please?"

"Sure." Tacey wasn't even sure she'd gotten the whole word out before the dinky piano music blared out of her phone. Sixty-six seconds later, it ended.

"Mr Lamont's earliest appointment is next Thursday at ten."

Less than two days before Matt expected her to surrender Rory. Talk about leaving things to the last minute…

Tacey closed her eyes. "I'll take it."

The receptionist then went on to explain that Mr Lamont charged a consulting fee for his time, including initial consultations like this one, and that Tacey would be expected to pay it in full before the meeting could take place…

By the time Tacey got off the phone, she'd given the receptionist every detail the woman had asked for, plus paid more than a day's takings just to secure a meeting with the guy. If the reviews all over the internet were true – both bad and good, depending on whether they were written by his clients or the clients' pissed off partners – he'd be cheap at twice the price.

Anything for Rory.

"Uh, Tacey? Do we have any more almond milk? Oh, and can you tell me if the gingerbread is vegan?" Rochelle called.

Tacey peeked into the café. The afternoon rush had arrived. "No to the gingerbread, because I used eggs…but the shortbread is vegan. I used olive oil spread instead of butter. I'll go see if there's any more almond milk in the cool room."

After a brief trip to the cool room, she

returned to the counter with an armload of almond milk and oat milk (just in case one of the vegans had a nut allergy), and didn't get another moment to think about anything other than coffee or food until a rosy sunset glow turned the building across the road pink. Then it was time to bundle Rory into the car, where Wystan was already waiting, before going home to make dinner and fall into bed, before starting all over again tomorrow.

TWENTY

"Once again, Miss Bell, I can't believe your luck. You must have the only pest-free building in the whole of Fremantle." The pest control guy held up his hands. "I don't just mean clean, either. Plenty of places are clean, and they still can't get rid of what's living in the walls. All these old buildings, and the port nearby…not to mention the backpackers down the road…the infestation got so bad over the summer that it overflowed into the police station. You're lucky you didn't get any of it here."

Tacey shuddered. She'd heard about the latest cockroach plague at the backpackers, which was why she always had regular inspections. How the backpackers remained in business when they had more rats than guests sometimes, she had no idea. But as long as the pests didn't come to the Shut Up Café, that was between the manager of the backpackers and the health inspector.

"What's your secret?" he asked.

His guess was as good as hers. Probably just luck, actually. But… "My housemate did a warding spell on the place when we first took over the café, because my sister found a dead cockroach upstairs and freaked out. We haven't seen another one since, so maybe the spell worked."

The guy snorted. "That's actually more believable than the story I heard from one of the backpackers. He's convinced the bugs were the Moth Man's familiars, and that to do anything to get rid of them would summon the Moth Man to curse the whole town with…was it zombies? I think it was zombies."

Tacey had to laugh at that. "Well, I won't deny that the Moth Man videos were taken from this very café, but I've never seen him, and if I saw him or any kind of bug army, you'd be the first person I'd call to get rid of them. I remember having pantry moths once at home when I was a kid. Those little maggoty caterpillars everywhere. Ugh, never again!"

He just shook his head. "Pantry moths are the hardest to prevent. They come in with your groceries, and unless you have time to freeze everything for a couple of weeks before you use it, every bag of flour is a risk." He tapped on his tablet screen. "When I get back to the office, I'll have one of our admin staff email you the final inspection report. Now, barring any unforeseen outbreak of pantry moths, I will see you again in six months." He waved as he headed out the door, only to have to stop to allow a guy with a loaded trolley to come in.

"Speak of the devil," Tacey heard him say as he walked away.

But Tacey was too busy dealing with the delivery to have time for anyone or anything else.

Finally the right flour had arrived.

"Put one bag on the counter in the kitchen for tomorrow morning, and stack the rest in the store room," she directed.

It took him four trips, but by the time his truck pulled away from the kerb, Tacey was almost ready to sing. After months of supply shortages, things were looking up.

TWENTY-ONE

"But I don't like chocolate muffins! Brown ones are yucky!" Rory shouted.

Tacey rubbed her eyes. First Disney princesses, now chocolate? Sometimes she wondered if Rory was a girl at all. "But yesterday you ate two chocolate muffins, and you wouldn't eat anything else." Not even dinner, which had turned into a screaming match, with Rory doing most of the screaming.

She was pretty sure Octavia had slipped her some food later, too, when they were watching TV.

"Mistress Tacey, I believe Miss Rory burned her mouth on one of the muffins yesterday. The chocolate inside was still liquid. Perhaps if you cut one in half so that it was definitely cool in the middle…" Wystan began.

Not only was he a better protector than Tacey was, he was already a better parent, too. Maybe Rory really would be better off with Matt. He might have better luck getting her to eat healthy food.

Tacey pulled out a different muffin. "This one's apple and cinnamon. It was one of the first batch I cooked, and it's definitely cool all the way through."

Rory perked up. 'Is it crunchy like an apple?"

Only because this one was slightly overdone. "It is on top," Tacey admitted.

"Yay!"

Tacey blew out a breath. Well, that was the

breakfast battle won. She wasn't looking forward to the lunch one.

Downstairs, the bell chimed to indicate someone had entered the café.

"I'll be back later with lunch. You be good for Wystan, okay?" Tacey said, hurrying down the stairs.

The woman who approached the counter looked vaguely familiar. Not a regular, but…

"What can I get you?" Tacey asked.

The woman wrinkled her nose. "Oh, I'm not here to order anything. I'm here to investigate a complaint. I'm Rachael Smythe, one of the Environmental Health Officers from the City of Fremantle. We've had a number of complaints this week about a cockroach infestation here."

Tacey couldn't help it. She laughed. "Oh, no, that's not us. You're looking for the backpackers. They're the ones with roaches. We had a pest control inspection only yesterday, and he didn't find a single thing. Not a roach or a rat or even a redback spider."

Maybe Callie's spell had actually worked. Seeing as the summoning spell in the cemetery had produced Wystan, it was possible that magic might exist after all. She couldn't wait to tell Callie, when she got home from that wedding.

The woman pulled a tablet out of her bag and began swiping at the screen. "This is the Shut Up Café, isn't it?"

"Yes…"

"All the complaints definitely state your café, not the backpackers. Oh, it looks like some of the complaints were filed by residents at the backpackers, but they said the bugs were here."

Tacey shook her head. "That's impossible. The pest control guy said there was nothing. It's all in the report."

"Show me, please."

Tacey led the way into the kitchen, where she'd left her laptop. "He said he was going to send it through…" But when she logged into her email account, there was nothing from the pest control company at all. "I'll have to call them and ask them to send it through again."

"You do that. In the meantime, can I take a look around?"

If she saw Wystan…but he'd hidden from the pest control guy yesterday, so he'd probably do the same today. Admittedly, she'd been able to warn him yesterday, while Rachael didn't look like she was going to give Tacey the chance to do that now. Tacey swallowed. Pissing off the health inspector never ended well, and she had no right to refuse. Unlike police officers, environmental health officers were allowed wherever they pleased, within their jurisdiction. "Sure," Tacey said, praying to any deity who was listening that Rachael would see the same as the guy yesterday. No pests, no gargoyles, and no problems.

The bell rang again, and Tacey was forced to go back to the counter to serve coffee to a stream of customers, so many that she almost forgot about the health inspector until Rachael cleared her throat.

Tacey handed over the last cappuccino and dusted her hands on her apron. "Yes?"

Rachael just shook her head. "Will you come with me, please?"

Dread curdled in Tacey's stomach, though she had no idea why. Unless Wystan was somehow a health code violation...

But Rachael didn't head upstairs. Instead, she ducked through the kitchen and out to the store room. She pushed the door open and backed away. "Explain this, please."

"What the f..." Tacey spluttered. The place was crawling with giant cockroaches, like something out of an Indiana Jones film. "None of these were here yesterday!"

Rachael nodded with apparent sympathy. "They never are. Look, I'll tell you what. This is your first offence, so I'll issue you with a warning. No fine this time. If you get this seen to immediately, like today, I might be able to avoid closing you down entirely, instead of just temporarily. I can come back on Friday to do a follow up inspection, and if there's evidence you're taking action, and this place is safe to serve food again, maybe you can open on the weekend."

Tacey gaped. For a long moment, she had no words. And then fury surged through her veins, and she had all the words. "I can't stay closed all week! Tomorrow. Come back tomorrow. They'll all be gone by then, just like they were yesterday, I swear."

Rachael frowned. "You do realise that if I come back tomorrow and they're still here, I'll have to close you down indefinitely, right? But Friday…"

"Tomorrow," Tacey insisted. "I'll call the pest control guy who was here yesterday and get him here today."

Five minutes and a desperate phone call later – during which Dave, the pest control guy, sounded as confused as Tacey felt – and Dave was already on his way.

Rachael didn't have time to wait for him, but she agreed to return first thing in the morning, to determine whether the café would be allowed to open tomorrow, or at all.

TWENTY-TWO

"Sorry it took me so long. Some idiot had rolled his truck on the freeway, and traffic was backed up halfway to Joondalup. Now, did you say you found a cockroach? It must have flown in from next door, because this place was cleaner than my mother-in-law's bathtub on rent inspection day." Dave marched in with a toolbag in hand.

Tacey hadn't been able to even look in the

store room. She really, really wanted to believe she was hallucinating. "The health inspector found a plague of cockroaches in the store room. See for yourself."

Dave raised his eyebrows, then strode off, muttering. The muttering turned to loud swearing when he found them.

Several hours later, when Dave announced that every last bug was dead, Tacey almost didn't want to go in to see the carnage. But Dave insisted.

"I told you, if any pests moved in, they'd have come in with your supplies. All it took was one bag of flour – this one." He nudged the offending sack with his foot.

Unlike the others, this one had been sliced open along the top. Then Tacey looked at it more closely.

"This didn't come in yesterday's delivery. It's the wrong flour. Strong flour. We got this stuff a month ago, because it was all the supplier had, but the muffins and cookies just weren't right. So I tossed out the one open bag we had, and sent the rest back. This bag was in the bins out the back. Someone must have brought it in here, full of bugs…" Tacey shuddered.

"Only if they filled it with roaches first. You might get a couple in a bag in the bins, or half a dozen, what with the plague they had next door, but this many? Someone filled that bag right up before they put it into your café," Dave said.

"One of the people from the backpackers?" That's where the complaints had come from, so someone over there must have known.

"Someone over there must really hate you, do to something like this," Dave said.

Tacey could only shake her head. "But they all get ten percent off here, if they show their key. I can't imagine why anyone over there would want to close this place down."

"Well, someone sure hates you, is all I can say," Dave said. He nodded at the window, now wide open to vent the noxious fumes from the store room. "You should get that latch fixed, too. It doesn't close properly. Anyone could come in that way."

That was probably how the sack of bugs had been brought in in the first place. Which made no sense, because Tacey had never opened that window. She'd tried when they first moved in, but it'd been jammed shut. Now, it looked like someone had taken to the latch with a chisel, chipping away decades of paint to reveal the timber frame beneath.

"Someone's really got a grudge there, if you ask me," Dave said. "Are you sure you don't have any enemies?"

Tacey opened her mouth to deny it, and then remembered Matt. He'd pranked the school canteen once with a bag of bugs when they'd changed the garlic bread recipe. He'd boasted about it to her in private, afterwards, because he'd been so proud of not getting caught.

Was he trying to torment her, now, too?

"Tacey?"

She shook her head. Dave had been talking

to her, and she'd been lost in her thoughts. She didn't have time for that. She needed to fix this, now. "Sorry?"

"I said, I've just asked the office to email yesterday's inspection report. I'll get today's one written up, and send it through tonight. Or would you prefer me to deliver it personally?"

Her heart swelled at such kindness. "The health inspector will be here at seven tomorrow morning, when we open. If you could be here then to tell her what you've seen, I'd be very grateful. I'd even throw in a free coffee and breakfast."

He perked up. "Do you make those bacon and egg muffins? Not the ones you get at Maccas, but the ones where it's just a little bit of bread around the outside, packed full of bacon and egg in the middle, all wrapped up in muffin paper?"

She hadn't for a while, but she'd happily make him a whole batch if he'd help her pass her health inspection tomorrow. "Absolutely."

"Then I'll see you at seven."

Dave departed, and Tacey finished the day's shut down, even though it wasn't even dinnertime yet. Tomorrow, she'd reopen and everything would be fine.

She trudged up the stairs to where Rory had spread out her markers all over the floor. Except they weren't markers in her game any more – each one had a voice and a different dastardly plan, or so it seemed. Rory was surprisingly good at villain voices.

"Miss Tacey, I've checked the entire building. There are no more vermin within the walls, or anywhere else," Wystan said, appearing from nowhere.

Tacey forced herself to nod. "Thank you. That means they really were only in the store room. Someone planted them there. If only we'd had a surveillance camera in the store room…" But they'd only had the one Wystan had broken, and that had been in the main café. The store room window opened onto the courtyard at the backpackers – which only the people staying at the hostel had access to. Matt wouldn't have been caught dead staying in somewhere like that. But who else could it have been? She could only shake her head. "I just need to put the dead bolts back on the back window, and then the sun should have set, so we can go home. We could even pick up some food on the way, instead of cooking. What do you want, Rory?"

She'd have asked Wystan, but he refused to eat anything she'd given him. Even her muffins, and she knew those were good.

"Chicky nuggies!" Rory shouted.

So much for eating healthy. But Tacey was too tired to argue. "Sure," was all she said, as she headed downstairs to dig out the drill.

TWENTY-THREE

Bell House was depressingly dark when Tacey pulled up outside. Octavia's car was notably absent, too. Another night alone, after she put Rory to bed and Wystan went up to stand watch on the rooftop. Alone in this isolated house, surrounded by bush, where anyone or anything could be hiding…

"There is no one here except us, mistress," Wystan said, as though reading her mind.

Tacey dared to breathe again. Of course Matt wouldn't be here. He wasn't the type to stalk her, or physically attack her. He was more into pranking, like the sack of cockroaches and the complaints to the health department. Now she thought about it, he'd probably made those reports himself, claiming to be different fake backpackers. He was probably at home in his parents' mansion by the river, sniggering into his expensive dinner, which he wouldn't have had to cook.

Enough about him. She was home, and she needed to get Rory fed and prepared for bed. "Okay, inside and wash up for dinner, please," she said as she stepped out of the car.

"I'm not hungry! Wystan said he could take me flying, just like the Mandalorian!" Rory jumped out, and began swooping around the car, with her arms outstretched like wings.

When had Mr Monster become Wystan to Rory? Tacey just shook her head. It didn't matter. Rory was not flying with him – not now, not ever. "Dinner first. Then, maybe after dinner, we'll see."

"But I've eaten my dinner, Mummy. No nuggies left!" Rory protested.

Tacey had heard that before, and she didn't believe it now, either. It wasn't until she'd unpacked the paper bags on the dining table that she found Rory was actually telling the truth. The torn open nuggets box was indeed empty, and all the cherry tomatoes were missing from Tacey's own salad, too.

"Can I fly now, Mummy, please?"

"I swear she will be as safe with me in the air as she is on the ground, Mistress Tacey," Wystan said from out on the veranda.

Tacey closed her eyes. She trusted him enough to guard Rory, but…humans weren't meant to fly. And Rory was already tired, which meant too much excitement would stop her going to sleep. Then again, if she threw one of her mighty tantrums because Tacey wouldn't let her fly, she wouldn't go to sleep, either…

"Allow me to show you, Mistress Tacey."

He peered through the front screen door, a hulking shadow that should have been scary, but she only found it reassuring. He could have ripped the door off its hinges, or punched through the screen with one blow, but he respected her rules of not allowing monsters in the house.

She was insane for even considering this.

Mum would scream at her for being so irresponsible, and how she'd rather die than put one of her daughters at risk like that.

Octavia would probably just grin and tell her to go for it.

Callie, on the other hand, would stand on the veranda with her arms folded, watching Wystan like a hawk as she threatened him with all manner of dire curses if anything bad happened to her family. Curses she could probably actually manifest, now Tacey thought about it.

If the other girls had been here, they'd have dragged her out to the veranda and insisted she do this, then clapped and cheered the whole time Wystan was in the air.

Tacey gritted her teeth, grabbed what remained of her dinner, and strode out to the veranda. "Okay, then. Show me," she said.

"YAY!" Rory cheered, climbing onto one of the outside chairs to watch.

TWENTY-FOUR

With Tacey standing in front of him, damn near vibrating with anger, Wystan almost backed down and changed his mind. In order to fly with her, he'd have to take her in his arms, and hold tight to her, when he hadn't touched a woman since his wife died.

"Come on, Mr Monster, make Mummy fly!" Rory cried.

Wystan closed his eyes. He could not

disappoint the child.

"Place your arms around my neck," he instructed.

Despite the cold winter air and the thick sweater she wore, he could still feel the heat of her body as she did as he asked.

He wanted to seize her around the waist, pressing her body tight against his, as he launched high into the air, but he feared such close contact would frighten her more than the flight. So, he lifted her like a new bride about to be carried across the threshold and gave a couple of lazy flaps, before he lifted them off the ground.

Her arms tightened around his neck as he slowly flew the length of the lawn, and back again, his feet almost skimming the grass, he flew so low. He did a second lap of the lawn, before returning to the veranda.

"You can let go now," he said.

Tacey blinked. "Right." A long moment later, she peeled her arms from around his neck and stepped away.

The loss of her warm weight hit him hard, where his heart had once been. He wanted to fly with her again. Higher, further, faster…holding her closer. Maybe even hold her for longer afterwards, if she'd let him. Another time, he promised himself. If she was willing.

Rory jumped up and down. "My turn! My turn!"

Tacey frowned, but she nodded. "All right. As long as you hold on tight, and are very careful, and you don't fly too high."

Wystan held his arms out to the little girl. Fearless Rory leaped into his embrace, hugging him tighter than her mother had.

He'd thought holding Tacey would be the biggest challenge, but Rory…between the way her whole face lit up, the giggles bubbling out of her mouth, and the trusting grip of her arms on him…it was like a dream. Like he was holding his own daughter, alive in his arms, for the very first time. Heaven, surely, and a heaven he did not deserve.

Unless by protecting Rory and Tacey, he might earn a place in heaven beside Effie.

Under Tacey's watchful gaze, he flew back and forth across the lawn, relishing every moment. Tacey could not have given him any greater gift, and he would be eternally grateful for it. He pitied the girl's father, who had never known such joy. Just as Wystan himself hadn't until this moment.

All too soon, Tacey rose from her seat, tucking the empty packaging that had held her dinner into the bag it had arrived in. "All right. Time for bed, Rory," she said gently.

Wystan landed carefully on the deck, leaning over to set Rory down on her own feet again. But she didn't let go until she'd landed two big, smacking kisses on each of his cheeks and thanked him, without any prompting from her mother.

Then she dashed inside, where Wystan knew he could not follow. But Tacey did, and his heart went with them.

TWENTY-FIVE

Rory yawned all the way to the bathroom, drooping as she brushed her teeth, and her eyes were already closing as her head touched the pillow. "Wasn't flying fun, Mummy?" she mumbled.

Tacey kissed her cheek. "It sure was." She wished Rory good night and closed the door behind her.

A sensible mother would go to the kitchen,

clean up the remains of their dinner, load the dishwasher, and maybe see if they needed to add anything to the shopping list. Do a load of laundry, so she could pop it in the dryer overnight.

But wasn't feeling sensible tonight. Sure, she'd fulfilled her motherly obligations, making sure Rory was safe and fed and went to bed, so now her time was her own. Well, within limits. She couldn't leave Rory alone in the house, so she could hardly do what the other twentysomethings she knew did, and go to the pub or something.

The pub was out. But there were some bottles of cider in the fridge, so she grabbed two and took them out to the veranda. The lights were still on out there, but Wystan's hulking shadow had disappeared. He'd gone up to the roof to stand watch.

"Want to come down and keep watch here for a minute, while we share a cider or two?" she called on impulse. Not too loud, because she wasn't sure what she'd do if he actually accepted her invitation, so it was probably for the best that he didn't.

Except…a massive shadow swept across the lawn, wheeling around far faster than he'd done with herself or Rory, and there he stood at the bottom of the steps, wings outstretched like Batman's worst nightmare.

But not hers.

She held out a cider bottle. "Want one?"

He folded his wings away and strode up the steps, but he didn't take the bottle. "No, thank you, Mistress Tacey. Thank you for allowing me to take Miss Rory flying. I believe she enjoyed herself."

"I should be thanking you. You tired her out so thoroughly, she's probably already dreaming about it." She frowned. "Why won't you accept any food or drink? I mean, you have to eat, right? If my cooking was bad, I'd be worried, but I've been running the Shut Up Café long enough to know there's nothing wrong with my cooking, so it can't be that. It's not like I'm not going to poison you or anything. The cider's still sealed. You can take your pick, and I'll drink the other bottle."

"I thank you for your offer of hospitality, always, but I have no need for sustenance. Gargoyles neither eat nor drink, for we are made of living stone. I cannot recall the last time I drank a pint of cider, but I am sure it was poorer quality than anything you have to offer."

Now he'd piqued her curiosity. Tacey cracked open a bottle and took a swig. "So you haven't always been a gargoyle?"

"Indeed I have not. I was once a man, as human as you."

All the little details she'd noticed and filed away as strange began to weave together. The way he referred to her car as a carriage. His insistence on using titles for herself and Rory, or his suggestions that they needed a male protector in their lives. Well, they probably did need him right now, but in general…

"How long have you been a gargoyle?" she asked carefully.

He shrugged. "I do not know. I awoke when you summoned me, as you see me now. Before that, I remember being a man."

"So you've only been a gargoyle for maybe a couple of weeks, and you can fly like you've been doing it forever. I bet birds wish they could do that." She drained the bottle of cider. "I wish I could do that." The words slipped out, almost of their own accord.

He raised his eyebrows. "I did not realise that you enjoyed flying."

She felt her cheeks heat, and was immensely grateful she was sitting in the shadows, where he couldn't see her blush. "It was all new to me. No man has ever carried me like a bride before, and it was also my first time flying."

"If you wish it, I will fly with you again. We were barely in the air for a minute or two, before Miss Rory claimed her turn. I would gladly fly with you for as long as you wish."

Temptation taunted her to accept. She'd let Rory go with him, and she'd been so, so safe. She knew Wystan wouldn't drop her, and just once, she wanted…she wanted…

"Yes, please."

TWENTY-SIX

Even as Wystan made the offer, he could see the refusal in Tacey's eyes. So when her lips said, "Yes, please," he wasn't sure if he'd heard right. It was one thing to hold a live child in his arms tonight, but a woman as well, for more than a moment…

Tacey clicked the lock on the door, so that Rory was secure inside. "Rory likes the Mandalorian, but when I was a kid, I preferred

Superman. I wanted to be Lois Lane, when he flies her up through the clouds to see the stars." She looked up at the clouds already sailing in from the west. There would be rain tomorrow, Wystan was sure of it, but it would be dry for some hours yet. Long enough to fly Tacey high enough to see what she desired.

He'd never dared to fly so high, but with her in his arms, he would dare anything. Especially if she commanded it.

"When you are ready, place your arms around my neck once more, and hold on tight," Wystan said.

"But not too tight. You still need to breathe," she said with a breathy little laugh as she curled her arms around his neck.

"I do not need to breathe, much like I do not need to eat or drink. I only need air to speak," he admitted. "And I have no need for sleep, either, so I can remain vigilant throughout both the day and night, to keep you safe."

"Sounds ideal. I think I'm even a bit jealous.

To not need to eat or sleep…think of all the time I'd have spare!" Tacey said. "Plus you can fly. I think I'd like to be a gargoyle."

"You would not say that if you'd spent most of this week, tortured by the enticing scents of coffee, muffins, cookies and all manner of treats I could not taste but could definitely smell, while I watched over Miss Rory in your café. You are a remarkably good cook, Mistress Tacey."

She laughed. "Says the man who's never tasted a single bite of anything I've cooked. And even I have my weaknesses. Fish, for example. I can cook the most complicated pastries – croissants, eclairs, tarts – but I cannot, for the life of me, cook a fillet of fish without it falling apart or burning."

Now it was Wystan's turn to laugh. "Whereas I fear fish is about all I can cook. Whole or filleted over a fire, or cut into chunks in a stew. During the last stages of my wife's pregnancy, she wanted to eat nothing but fish, and I, as a good husband, would go and catch it for her, and cook it as she directed. We probably would have died of starvation on the beach here in the colony if not for my Effie's cravings for fish."

Tacey stiffened, her body no longer pressed against his. "And what does your wife think about you guarding Rory and me, instead of being home with her?"

Oh, if only he knew the answer to that. He hoped she'd be somewhere with their daughter, where such cares no longer mattered. "Effie died in childbirth almost two hundred years ago. There isn't a day I don't miss her, or wish I could ask for her insight on a thousand different things. She probably would have liked you and doted on Rory, for she had the biggest heart for such a small woman. I'd have given my life for hers, or our daughter's, but death took her so swiftly, I never had the chance." He was fortunate that gargoyles could not cry, for he was perilously close to doing so, and what would Tacey think of a weak, weeping protector?

"I'm sorry, Wystan. That must have been terrible for you, to lose your family like that. I can't even imagine what I'd do if I lost Rory…" She swallowed. "Please, could we go flying now? Before I chicken out or say anything even more stupid, and you decide this is a terrible idea."

He chuckled. "You are no coward, Tacey Bell. In fact, I think you might just be the bravest woman I have ever known."

She snorted. "You haven't met Octavia or Callie, then. The things they get up to…I mean, summoning you was Callie's idea. I never would have even considered it if I'd known the spell would summon an actual monster."

"Yet it is you, and not one of the other women, who is standing here now, with your arms about a monster's neck, asking him to take you flying. You trusted me with your daughter, the most precious person in the world to you, even though you know I am a monster." He leaned in, pressing his face to her throat, and growled, "Aren't you afraid of me, Tacey?"

A shiver darted through her body, yet her grip around his neck only tightened. "I should be."

Her voice was throaty, huskier than normal. He raised his head to meet her gaze and he was lost.

An eternity later, he surfaced, his lips pressed against her mouth, his tongue entwined with hers…and his hands gripping her hips so firmly it was a mercy there was so much clothing between them, or he might have ravished her.

She broke the kiss, for he was powerless to resist. "I'm sorry. I need to…goodnight." And then she was gone, locking the door behind her.

Damn and blast and…why were the pants of this time so damn tight?

Grumbling, Wystan headed up to the roof, where the night breeze could cool his ardour and clear his head, so that he could focus on keeping her safe.

And most definitely not think about what she might wear to bed tonight, in her bedchamber below.

No, not thinking about her at all.

TWENTY-SEVEN

"Aren't you afraid of me?"

Half the night, she couldn't help but rehash those moments in her head. The way he'd growled against her neck, sending a shiver right down her spine into her core, heating her whole body from the inside out. And then she'd kissed him, god only knew why, and it had been the hottest, most perfect kiss of her life.

She'd come to her senses when she'd realised the hard length pressing against her belly was as eager for her as she was for him, and she'd been a hair's breadth from wrapping her legs around him and impaling herself on him, clothing be damned.

Crazy monkey sex with a monster on her veranda in winter, for fuck's sake. Was there anything more insane? If anyone knew she'd even thought about it, they'd take Rory away from her for sure, and they'd be right to, because her mental state right now did not resemble that of a responsible parent at all.

Three times she'd had to take care of herself, she'd been so hot just thinking about it. Better than inviting the monster into her bed, no matter how much she wanted to.

So it was no wonder she felt like absolute shit the next morning when she opened her eyes in the predawn darkness.

"Mummy! Can we go flying again tonight?" Rory burst into the room and bounced on the bed, so full of energy it was obscene.

"We'll see," Tacey said, as she forced herself out of bed. She had a health inspector to convince, and a café to open.

She wasn't sure what to say to Wystan this morning. That kiss and what had almost happened between them…no, Rory did not need to know any of it. Tacey wished she didn't remember it.

Wystan appeared supremely unruffled, as though last night's kiss had meant nothing to him. The guy was made out of stone – maybe he didn't feel lust, or love, or…anything at all. Lucky.

Tacey's morning passed in a haze of coffee, and a few more muffins than were good for her. Rachael the health inspector and Dave the pest control guy turned out to be colleagues who'd worked together in Esperance a while back, and when he explained the roach situation, she took him at his word, not only happy to let the café open as normal that day, but to accept coffee and a muffin so she could catch up with Dave at a table in the corner before she was due in the office.

Shaking her head at the weirdness of her world, Tacey tried to concentrate on the cappuccino she was supposed to be drawing art on. Maybe she should just stick to using stencils with cocoa powder today, because abstract art was definitely not one of her strengths.

If Ben and Rochelle saw the bird that was supposed to be a rabbit on the last coffee, they'd have laughed themselves sick, and rightly so.

Good thing Ben wasn't in the café during the day. Definitely a night owl, that boy.

TWENTY-EIGHT

"Will you save me from the monster that tried to kill my mummy, Mr Monster?" Rory asked, not looking up from her drawing. "He has lots of bugs, Mummy said, because he brought a whole bag of them here and they went everywhere. I don't like bugs, and I especially don't like them if Mummy isn't there to smack them." She clapped her hands as if to demonstrate her mother's bug-smacking technique.

Wystan winced. It smote his heart to think of a girl growing up, believing her father to be a monster. Yet the more he saw and heard about the man, the more he was inclined to believe Tacey was right.

"You have to save me. I heard Mummy talking to Grandma on the phone last night, when I was supposed to be asleep, and she said if the lawyer wouldn't help her, she'd have to give me to him. I don't want to go. I want to stay with Mummy. And you."

His heart, if he still had one, was getting a workout today. The little girl didn't know what she was asking, but it was sweet that she liked him enough to want him to stay. Heaven knew he wanted to, but he wasn't sure how much time he had. He was here to protect Rory and Tacey, but he had no idea if that meant forever or just for a short time, the duration of a current threat. When he was done, perhaps he'd be allowed to die again, for surely he had already, to have woken in a grave, and he'd be reunited with Effie and the baby.

He'd miss Rory and Tacey, of course, but at least he'd know they were safe, thanks to him. Except…would they be? If they were his family, he would not rest until he was reunited with them. Monster or not, surely Rory's father would want the same?

Which meant that he would likely be Tacey's protector for some time. Perhaps her lifetime, or Rory's. The thought warmed his no longer beating heart. Perhaps there might be another kiss from Tacey in his future, though she seemed to have either regretted or forgotten their first one.

Still, if he had a lifetime by her side, there would be other chances. Rory would ask him to fly with her again, and he would offer to take Tacey up as well. Up above the clouds to see the stars, like this super man she had spoken of.

Something tugged insistently on his arm. For such a small girl, Rory had surprising strength. "You gotta promise, Mr Monster!"

Wystan took her hand in both of his. "Rory Bell, I promise to protect you with all of my power."

Rory cheered, pulling out of his grasp to dance about the room. "Yay! Can we fly now?"

If only. "Not until it is dark, and only if your mother agrees," he said.

He doubted she would, for Tacey had scarcely spoken three words to him all day, but it didn't matter, for by the time the sun had set, Rory had forgotten all about flying and was more excited about having pizza for dinner, whatever that was.

TWENTY-NINE

Silence reigned between Tacey and Wystan right up until the morning of her lawyer appointment. She was congratulating herself on what was looking to be a good day when her phone rang.

"Hi, Mum," she said.

"I'm so sorry, Tacey. Your dad was home with what he thought was food poisoning from a sandwich he bought at work yesterday, but it looks like I've got the bug, too. I won't be able to come and pick up Rory today."

Oh God. No way did she want Rory to catch it. Between worrying about Rory getting dehydrated and cleaning up the mess, Tacey wouldn't be able to escape catching the bug, too, and…

But she had the lawyer's appointment today. She could hardly bring Rory along. There were some things a kid didn't need to know, and dealing with child custody lawyers was right up there.

Her mind whirling, Tacey managed to mumble something sympathetic and wish Mum a speedy recovery before the call ended.

If it weren't the middle of the day, she'd consider asking Wystan to watch her. He'd watched over her upstairs while Tacey was working in the café these last couple of weeks, but she'd always been here, too. Plus there was Wystan's weird allergy to sunlight…

She should have asked Octavia instead of Mum. Sure, Octavia wasn't a morning person, seeing as she stayed up most of the night doing who knew what on her computer, but if she'd asked her, Octavia would've been there. For her and for Rory.

Not that she'd seen much of Octavia at all since that night at the cemetery.

Tacey considered calling her, but there was no way Octavia would be awake yet, and if she was asleep, she wouldn't even answer a text until lunchtime. Too late for the appointment, anyway.

The morning rush started early, and went through until Tacey had to leave – she didn't even have a moment to call anyone, and now it was too late.

She'd just have to take Rory with her, and hope the lawyer had a spare desk or table where Rory could draw or something. Surely a family lawyer would have somewhere suitable for kids. He'd deal with heaps of single parents who didn't have babysitters to help.

Tacey trudged up the stairs, dread rising with every step. She didn't want to take Rory to the lawyer. Didn't want her to know about the possible custody battle. It wasn't fair on Rory.

"Rory, I know Grandma was supposed to come and pick you up for a bit, but she's sick, so you'll have to come with me to my meeting instead," Tacey said.

"Do I have to?" Rory whined. "Wystan was going to help me with my drawing. I can't get his wings right, so he promised he'd do them for me."

"Maybe this afternoon, when we get back," Tacey said. "Come on, pack up your stuff. You can take your things with you, and maybe do some more drawing while I'm in my meeting. Then you can show Wystan when you get back."

Rory whined a bit more, but she did as she was told. Within minutes, she had her shoes and her backpack on and she was headed down the stairs.

"Ooh, Mummy, these are perfect wings," Rory said. "Come look!"

When Tacey reached the bottom of the stairs, Rory was nowhere in sight. It took her a minute to find her, standing on one of the chairs at Ben's usual table, examining his art on the wall.

"We don't stand on chairs, we sit on them," Tacey chided.

"Yes, Mummy, but I need to see these!"

"You can look at them later. Right now we need to go," Tacey said.

"But the man just put them on the wall. I'm not allowed to put pictures on the wall, but he said he's allowed!"

No, Tacey did not need a new tantrum to deal with. Rory was too big to carry out to the car while she was screaming. She wasn't a two-year-old any more. "Which man?" she asked. Because this was Ben's gallery, as her artist in residence, and no one else was allowed to pin art to her walls. If someone thought they were going to just come in here and steal Ben's job, they'd be out on their ear before they could blink.

Rory pointed to the customer at the counter. "The one kissing Auntie Rochelle!"

Ben. Tacey blinked. Ben, in the daytime? Didn't he have a day job, which was why he could only come to the café after dark?

"Tacey. Rory," Ben said, doing that chin lifting greeting thing the students at the high school did.

"What are you doing here?" Tacey asked.

Ben grinned. "Would you believe I'm getting coffee and a muffin? I had nothing to do today, and seeing as Rochelle is working, I thought I might keep her company. It looks like my table's free, and I brought my sketch books, so as long as you don't mind…" He winked. "I can always go out back and do the dishes to earn my keep, if a few new sketches aren't enough."

"Mummy, look at these wings!"

Tacey didn't have time to look at sketches, even Ben's. "Maybe later. Uncle Ben's going to be very busy drawing, so we should go and leave him to it now."

Ben set his satchel on the table, beside his coffee. "I don't mind if she sits with me. Hey, maybe I could teach you to draw wings just like that, if you want. If you keep practicing every day, by the time you're grown up, you'll be a better artist than me!'

"Please, Mummy? I don't want to go! I want to draw wings with Uncle Ben!"

If it were any normal day, Tacey might allow it. After all, Ben was hardly a monster, not like Wystan. He'd been Rochelle's sort of bodyguard the whole time she'd been hiding here from her abusive ex. And she'd trusted Rochelle to keep an eye on Rory, and Rochelle would be here…

"I don't know how long I'll be out. I might be a few hours," Tacey hedged.

Ben shrugged and flipped open his sketchbook. "Do you have your own paper, Rory, or do you want to borrow some of mine?"

Rory set her bag down and began pulling out art supplies. "I have everything I need right here."

Ben chuckled. "It's almost as if you knew I'd be coming in today. Well, art class is in session, I guess."

"Are you sure?" Tacey asked. "If she's any trouble, just get Rochelle to call me and I'll come right back. If I'm not back by lunchtime and Rory gets hungry, order some lunch for her. For both of you. On the house."

Ben snorted. "Rory won't be any trouble. We're going to draw until we get hungry, and then we're going to have the best sandwiches in that cabinet over there, and we'll be right here when you get back. No worries."

Tacey was torn. Sure, Ben seemed like the ideal babysitter, a gift from heaven at just the right moment, but… "You can't let her leave the café. She has to stay right here, in this building. Nowhere else. Have you ever taken care of kids before?"

Ben gave her a mock salute. "Right. No trips to the brothel on Bannister Street."

Tacey blinked. "No…what?" She couldn't

possibly have heard that right.

Ben just laughed. "We'll be fine, Tacey. Like Rory said, we're going to be drawing wings. Go out, enjoy yourself. See you when you get back."

Tacey glanced at her watch. If she didn't leave now, she'd be late. And she did trust Ben and Rochelle… "All right. See you when I get back," she said, and forced herself to march out the door to her car.

It wasn't until she was halfway to the lawyer's office that she realised she'd never actually introduced Ben to Rory. How did he know her name?

Telling herself Rochelle must have mentioned her to him, Tacey just shook her head and kept driving. The sooner she engaged this lawyer's services, the sooner she could be more secure about Rory's future. No leaving her with a monster like Wystan. Better yet, if she no longer needed Wystan to protect them from Matt, then she could unsummon him (however you did that) and she'd never have to think about that kiss ever again.

THIRTY

An hour and twenty minutes, she'd been kept waiting. She'd chewed off all her lipstick, and even started biting her nails. Sure, the view of the river out the window of the high rise office where Lamont and Partners did business was real pretty, but she wanted to see the lawyer, not the ferries crossing and recrossing the damn river.

Worse, every minute she was away from

Rory, she imagined all manner of terrible things happening to her. She might reach for Ben's coffee and spill it on herself. Some crazy person might try to hold up the café, and hold her hostage. She might throw another tantrum and scare away all the customers, and Ben and Rochelle wouldn't know what to do. Or Matt might come into the café and take her while Tacey was here and when she got back, Rory would be gone...

"Miss Bell?"

Tacey glanced up, to meet the eyes of the perfectly coiffed and made up receptionist. "Uh, yeah?"

"Mr Lamont will see you now."

Tacey expected Dominic Lamont to actually appear, to shake hands or something, but the receptionist just got up and beckoned for Tacey to follow her down the corridor. Not only was there a sway in the woman's step that made her dress float around her like water caressing every perfect curve, but she wore heels so high, they'd have broken Tacey's ankles in three steps.

Tacey mentally shook herself, then fixed her gaze on the receptionist's pert bottom. Tacey might not look like a model, but she could kick this woman's arse at cooking. She could make better cakes and muffins and cookies and coffee…ha, this girl probably hadn't eaten any of those things since primary school.

Feeling a tiny bit better, she stepped into the kind of office she could live in.

The corner office was as big as her café, only two of the walls were entirely glass, looking out over the river.

"Mr Lamont, this is Tacita Bell," the receptionist said, before she sashayed out.

Tacey had to admire the woman – she'd even gotten the pronunciation right.

"Sit down, Miss Bell," came a deep voice from behind her.

Tacey forced her gaze away from the window.

Dominic Lamont looked just like his picture on the website. Big and dark, like he'd be able to find work as a bodyguard or a bouncer if he hadn't chosen to practice law. Hell, he probably intimidated the opposition just by looking at them.

Even Matt would hesitate to cross him.

With a grin on her face, she perched on the nearest chair. "Hi, I'm here to discuss representation in a custody case over my daughter. Her father, who tried to kill us both before she was born, just got out of prison and is threatening to apply for full custody of her. I need your help to make sure he doesn't succeed."

For a long moment, Lamont just stared at her. Dark eyes seemed to read her very soul, like he was the devil himself.

If she hadn't faced a monster like Wystan every day, Tacey might have flinched. Might have lowered her gaze.

But Lamont was just a man. A lawyer, but also just a man. He didn't scare her. She did hope he could scare Matt and the magistrate, though. That's who mattered. So she gritted her teeth and stared right back.

"If I'd wanted to have a staring contest, I'd have stayed home with my daughter. She doesn't charge by the hour," Tacey snapped.

Lamont just laughed. And laughed, and laughed. Finally, he wiped his eyes and said, "I can see why he was convicted. You make a very compelling witness. Even I almost believe you, and I know the truth."

Tacey's thoughts whirled. What was he on about? She was telling the truth.

"You don't believe Matt tried to kill me? He tampered with the brakes on that car of his, then borrowed my car so I'd have to drive his. If I hadn't been so cautious backing out of the driveway, I wouldn't have even noticed anything was wrong, and I probably would have gone careening over the cliff around the corner from his house, right into the river. Even when I talked to the mechanic who usually takes care of his car, I didn't believe Matt could have done it, until he showed me where the brakes had been cut. He's the one who called the police, who wanted to know if Matt had any enemies. When Matt wasn't the target, it was me."

Lamont just shook his head. Pityingly. The same way Mum had when she'd heard about Matt's arrest. Mum had never liked Matt, she'd said.

"I'm sure all your theatrics went down very well on the magistrate in the initial trial, but a lot's happened in the last six years, while you've been playing mother and baking cakes. Your made up sob story won't work in the Family Court. Not after Matt's gotten himself a decent lawyer who could launch a proper appeal, and he's been cleared of all charges. In fact, it'll only help his case. With your mental health issues and unsuccessful suicide attempt in his car when you found out you were pregnant and he wouldn't marry you, it's no wonder you blamed him for your own problems. Spouting that story now the courts have cleared him, you'll only come across as delusional, which will make my job almost too easy."

Tacey's mouth wouldn't seem to close. "What…what do you mean?" Delusions, attempted suicide, mental health issues? "Matt asked me to marry him the moment he found out I was pregnant. He insisted I come to live with him in his parents' house so he could take care of me until the baby came…" That's why she'd found it so hard to believe he'd wanted to kill her. Well, until the police had discovered the life insurance policy he'd taken out on her. Then she'd lost her illusions, and realised the truth.

So why was Lamont calling her delusional now?

He laughed again. "Miss Bell, I could listen to you spin stories all day, but I'm a very busy man and my time is valuable. You came here for legal advice, and I will give it to you. Give up the case. Give your daughter to her father, and consider yourself lucky he didn't file charges against you for framing him for attempted murder. If you wish to take this matter to court, you will lose, and likely end up locked up yourself. Only you'll go to a prison for the criminally insane, where you'll never see the outside world again."

Maybe she was delusional. She couldn't possibly have heard this lawyer say such a thing. She was as sane as anyone. Well, there was Wystan, but he definitely wasn't a delusion, even if she wished he was.

She wouldn't have imagined kissing a monster…

The receptionist had appeared again, magically summoned by Lamont.

"See Miss Bell out," he said, dismissing her with a flick of his fingers.

Tacey jumped to her feet. "No! I'm here to hire you to help me keep my daughter, not tell me to give her to Matt. If you think I'm going to hand my daughter over to the man who tried to kill me, you're as crazy as he is. I'll tell everyone what you said, and you'll be sorry!"

Lamont didn't seem the slightest bit concerned. "Take Miss Bell down to the lobby, and make sure security know not to allow her in the building again. Not only has she threatened me, but she's spreading lies about our newest partner. As if I'd believe her over my son's best friend! Ha, wait until Matt hears this one. He'll piss himself laughing for sure."

The puzzle pieces clicked together, and hit critical mass in Tacey's brain. "You mean Matt works here? For a law firm? When he's a convicted criminal? That's not possible!"

Lamont wagged a finger at her. "If only I'd been in the country for his initial trial. Sadly, I didn't hear about it until the graduation ceremony Matthew and Samuel should have attended together. When I asked Samuel where Matt was, only then did I discover he was languishing in prison. Poor boy had finished his whole degree behind bars and didn't even get out in time for the ceremony! Of course, I called in a few favours to see him cleared of all charges, and was only too happy to offer him a job. When he asked for my advice on getting custody of the child you'd stolen from him, I even offered to represent him. I couldn't allow his daughter to grow up in a cockroach infested café that's also a fire hazard waiting to happen. Now, get out. Before I call the Child Protection Office myself."

Tacey's mouth opened and closed, but no sound came out. She wasn't sure how she made it out the door, or down to the lobby, or even out to her car.

Lamont might not be the devil, but somehow she'd ended up in hell anyway.

THIRTY-ONE

True to his promise to both Tacey and Rory, Wystan drifted downstairs to the café, hidden within the walls, but near enough to see and hear.

Tacey had entrusted her daughter to a boy. A shiftless layabout who drew countless pictures with little care for the cost of paper or ink. Much like Rory did, but the difference was that the boy was nearly a man grown, one who should be learning a useful trade instead of drawing pretty pictures.

It hurt that Tacey trusted this boy more than she did Wystan himself to take care of her daughter. Had Wystan not protected her for these last two weeks? Yet Tacey had always been nearby, or at least near enough to hear him shout if he'd needed to raise the alarm that she or her daughter was in danger.

But this gangly boy...

Wystan resolved to stay as close as possible to Rory, while still remaining hidden, until Tacey returned.

"What is that you're drawing? Is it the Moth Man?" the boy asked.

Rory frowned. "No. Moth Men don't exist, Mummy said. Not outside of people's imaginations."

The boy laughed. "Oh, Tacey might be surprised at how many monsters do actually exist. Even the Moth Man. Did you know Rochelle filmed a video of him outside this very café?"

"I think he looked more like Batman. And

he disappeared into the wall. Batman can't do that. But gargoyles can." She tapped her picture. "Only I can't do the wings right."

The boy straightened in his seat. "And what do you know about gargoyles, little Rory?"

She glared at the boy like she thought he was a complete idiot. Wystan couldn't help but grin. "Sunlight hurts them, and they can hide in the walls. They can fly, too, because they have wings. Great big leathery ones like a pterodactyl." She threw her pencil down on the table. "But I can't draw them right, Uncle Ben. You do it."

"How about I draw the lines in lightly with my pencil, just to get you started, and you trace over them before you colour them in? And then the next time, we can both draw wings together, each on our own page."

"Okay." Rory shoved her sketchpad across the table to Ben.

"See, wings are actually just like big hands. They have bony bits just like fingers, here and here and here, and then claws on the corners, in case he needs to protect himself. He must be inside, or somewhere it's not too windy, to have his wings spread out like this, because that's how he catches the breeze to lift off the ground when he wants to fly."

Rory frowned. "He needs bigger claws. He's not just protecting himself. He's protecting people from monsters. Because that's what gargoyles do. They protect people." She took her pad back and began to extend the claws with angry strokes that dug deep into the paper.

She was too intent on her drawing to notice the calculating look Ben gave her, making him look far older than his years, before he was back to the carefree boy Wystan had taken him for. "Did your mummy tell you all that about gargoyles?"

Rory shook her head, not looking at him. "No. Wystan, the gargoyle who promised to protect me did. He turned to stone once when Mummy opened the blinds, but we covered him up and he turned back to himself again when I closed the blinds. He can't eat food, but he says if he could, he'd like to live on Mummy's muffins because they smell so delicious."

Wystan felt Ben's eyes on him, which couldn't be possible. No ordinary man could see through walls to where he was hiding.

Unless Ben was no ordinary man…

"Your protector sounds like he has very good taste. I'd like to meet Wystan some day. I would also like to eat nothing but your mum's muffins. But my mother always told me I should eat more fruit and vegetables and meat, not muffins, so we probably shouldn't have those for lunch. Did you know that Rochelle doesn't just make the prettiest coffee, but she can make a sandwich with almost anything? Just look at all of these!"

Rory wandered over to the counter to peer into the sandwich cabinet. "I want this one." She pointed at a roll bigger than her forearm, stuffed full of turkey, lettuce and cherry tomatoes. This was the Christmas in July special for today, Wystan knew, for he'd watched Tacey make them.

"Wow, you must really be hungry. Two of those, then, please, Rochelle. What do you want to drink, Rory?"

"Mummy always makes me a milkshake for lunch," Rory lied.

Wystan almost corrected her, because Tacey only ever made her a milkshake if there were no customers at the counter and she had time at lunch, which had happened exactly once in the whole time he'd known her.

But Rochelle was already nodding, like she'd done this a thousand times before. "Milk and ice cream, but no syrup, right, Rory?"

"Yup!" The girl grinned.

"No worries. I'll bring it all over when it's ready. I know where your table is," Rochelle said as she bustled about behind the counter.

Rory took Ben's hand and led him back to the table covered in art supplies. "Now you can teach me how to draw wings."

"And I want to hear everything you know

about gargoyles," Ben replied.

Rory giggled. "Don't you know about gargoyles? They're from olden times, in Scotland, so they don't know much about electricity and TV and things. Wystan didn't even know how to turn on the light until I showed him the switch!"

"I'm from Scotland. We didn't have light switches in our house, either, when I was growing up," Ben said. "To turn off the light, we had to blow out a candle."

"Really?" Rory's eyes were wide with wonder.

"Yep, really." Ben reached up and pinned his latest drawing to the wall. "Now, wings."

He kept on talking, but Wystan stopped listening. Instead, he shifted position until he was in a place where he could see the gallery of pictures that he'd never paid much attention to before.

Most of them were sketches of staff and customers in the café. There were plenty of Rochelle, but the latest one stopped him in his tracks.

This sketch showed a table just like the one they sat at now, with a little girl intent on the paper in front of her. But instead of Ben sitting beside her, he'd drawn a gargoyle with his wings folded behind him, with a cup of coffee in one hand and a muffin in the other.

Wystan would have given anything for the picture to be true. To sit down with them, instead of watching from the walls. At least he could watch, though, for when the sandwiches arrived, she insisted on stealing all of Ben's tomatoes, and she refused to give them back. He'd never laughed so hard in his life.

Man or boy or whatever Ben actually was, he was no match for Tacey's wily six-year-old. A girl he intended to protect like she was his own, for as long as fate would allow it.

THIRTY-TWO

Tacey wasn't sure how she got from the lawyer's office back to the café, though she must have driven. All she could think about was how she was going to lose Rory, because of Matt and that arsehole lawyer and all fucked up old boys club networks and nepotism and…and…

"Look what Uncle Ben and me drew!" Rory squealed, holding up a picture that was mostly grey.

Tacey mumbled something that she hoped sounded admiring, before she dragged her feet to the store room to take inventory before she placed next week's order. The weekend's supplies would arrive in the morning, and they were particularly low after a busy couple of weeks. Between the busyness and those bloody cockroaches, the store room was almost empty. Next, she headed for the cool room, then the freezer.

She placed the order in a daze, having to go back twice to check she'd counted right. It wasn't until she stepped out of the freezer a second time that she heard the piercing beep that couldn't possibly be…

"Fire," she said dully, marching toward the fire extinguisher. She'd trained often enough. Pull the pin, aim at the base of the fire and squeeze…she just had to find the fire.

The café was full of wide-eyed people, staring at her and each other as they pressed their hands over their ears to drown out the noise.

"Make it stop, Mummy!" Rory wailed, barely audible over the din.

The kitchen was clear, with no sign of any smoke to set off the screeching alarm. Then why…???

She stomped toward the alarm, picking up a tea towel to swat the stupid thing. Only to find she was stirring eddies into a cloud of smoke.

Smoke coming from under the store room door…

For fuck's sake.

She grabbed the door knob, then recoiled as the bloody thing was red hot. Remembering the tea towel, she used that instead.

The room was full of smoke, with flames all over the floor. Which made no sense, because there'd been nothing to burn.

None of this made any sense.

A shadow came barrelling out of nowhere, shoving her aside and leaping into the flames.

What kind of idiot…?

Remembering the fire extinguisher, Tacey

grabbed it and let loose, spraying everything in the store room until nothing came out. The breeze through the broken window blew smoke and fumes right back at her, making her cough. She dropped the now useless extinguisher and used the tea towel to cover her mouth and nose as she tried to wave away some of the noxious fumes so she could see.

It took twenty minutes of running every exhaust fan in the kitchen to air the place out before she dared to enter the store room again.

And gasped.

Wystan lay spread eagled on the floor, one wing in tatters like an umbrella that'd been through a hailstorm. He wasn't moving.

"Wystan? Are you all right?" she asked. Of course, she already knew the answer, but maybe, just maybe…

"Fine," he grumbled, rising up onto all fours before lumbering to his feet. Debris crunched under his hands and feet. No, broken glass, likely from the window. He turned around and…

Tacey had to look away. His pants had not survived the fire, either. She thrust the tea towel at him, though it wasn't likely to cover much more than the essentials, and barely even those.

There was that old bag of chef's whites in the bathroom that the previous owners had left behind. Something in there might fit him…

Tacey dug through it feverishly until she found a pair of pants and a shirt that would be big enough to cover his wings.

When she came back to hand him the clothes, though, she found him holding half a broken bottle.

"Someone started the fire by throwing a bottle of lamp oil through your window," he said.

Arson? Who would…

She barely had to think before she had her answer. Matt's lawyer friend had mentioned the café being a fire hazard waiting to happen. He must have heard it from Matt, who'd set out to deliberately burn the place down. He was going to take Rory from her, and her livelihood…hell, they both could have died in the fire.

Fuck Matt and the lawyer who busted him out of prison. He wasn't going to get away with this, either.

"I need to call the police," Tacey said.

THIRTY-THREE

"Who's this?"

When Tacey went back into the café, she found Ben staring intently at Wystan. Almost like he was sizing him up for a sketch. Or a fight, Tacey wasn't sure.

"This is Wystan. He's…here for additional security," Tacey said. Probably not the best thing to say to her artist in residence cum security guard. "And to help out in the kitchen." She probably should have said that in the first place, what with him wearing chef's whites and all.

But Ben didn't seem to be offended at all. He just nodded thoughtfully. "How long have you been in the protection business, Wystan?"

Almost like he already knew him. But that wasn't possible…was it?

"He's been helping me out for about a week now," Tacey said.

More nodding. "So what's he protecting you from?"

Tacey felt her cheeks grow hot. "Nothing you need to worry about. I wouldn't want you and Rochelle mixed up in any of this."

"You helped put the fire out?" Ben asked.

Wystan nodded. "It's safe now. I should help clean up…"

"No! We have to wait for the police. Forensics, maybe," Tacey said.

"I'll go wait in the car, then," Wystan said.

"Can I go with him, Mummy?" Rory asked.

"No, I need you to stay here. The police are

coming, and they might take a while. Maybe…you should go upstairs for a bit? I'll let you know when it's time to go," Tacey said.

Ben rose. "I'll go up with her, to open a few windows to help clear the smoke."

"I should go with her. You've been taking care of her all day. I can't thank you enough, even if the appointment was a waste of time. I should pay you for babysitting. I don't even know how much…" Tacey stammered.

Ben chuckled. "Actually, Rory's quite the little muse. While we were drawing this afternoon, she gave me the most amazing idea for a comic strip. I've been sketching ideas down for most of the afternoon. If anything, I should be paying you…or her." He strode up the stairs. "Looks like your police have arrived."

Sure enough, two officers were standing outside the door on the footpath outside.

THIRTY-FOUR

"Miss Bell, do you have any enemies? Anyone who might wish to harm you, or your business?" one of the police officers asked, while his partner was busy examining the store room.

Tacey blew out a frustrated breath. "Only my ex, Matt. Matthew Masters. He's demanding sole custody of our daughter and threatening that I'll regret it if I don't hand her over." But she wouldn't, she decided. No matter what Matt or his arsehole of a lawyer said, she knew Matt had tried to kill her in the past, and between the cockroaches and now this Molotov cocktail, he was trying to destroy her again now. No way was she going to let him win.

"Do you have an address for Mr Masters?"

Tacey recited the address of Matt's parents' riverfront mansion, the place with rolling lawns she'd rolled across when she'd jumped out of his sabotaged Holden HR Special. He probably still had the car, for it had only taken a few scratches to the tomato-red paint when it had hit the neighbours' hedge.

God, she'd be living there with him, if he hadn't tried to kill her. Rory would be running around on those lawns…

But no. Rory probably wouldn't have been allowed to play in the manicured gardens Arnold Masters had spent every spare moment grooming, though they were likely managed by a gardener now. Even if Christine Masters was no longer there to disapprove of anything that disrupted her perfect life, Matt had been too deeply indoctrinated in his mother's rules to ever break them.

The officer tucked his tablet away as his partner emerged from the kitchen. "All done?" The other officer nodded. "Well, we'll be going, Miss Bell. We'll send these samples down to the lab, and see if we can have a chat with Mr Masters. Meanwhile, you might want to board up that window. If we find anything, we'll be in touch."

Tacey nodded and walked them out.

When she re-entered the café, she realised the place was empty except for herself and Rochelle – not a customer in sight. Tacey sighed. "We should probably close up early. You and Ben go home, while I see to fixing that window…" For the second time in as many weeks.

Ben pounded down the stairs. "Did you say you needed a carpenter? I've spent a bit of time in the building trades. Show me where your tools are and I can take care of your window. You need to get Rory home before she falls asleep and you have to carry her down those stairs."

Some mother she was. Rory could've died in the fire, and Tacey had completely forgotten she was even here. "Yes. Rory. Are you sure? I can pay you…"

Ben just laughed. "I don't need your money, Tacey. Keep it for yourself and your daughter. It sounds like you'll need it more than I do, especially the way Rory goes through art supplies. She's a good kid, that one. You get her home and keep her safe, now."

There was a note of command in Ben's tone that she'd never heard before, and Tacey found herself nodding obediently. He was a young street artist, and Rochelle's boyfriend, but there was something in his eyes that spoke of more. Like when he'd stared down Wystan, as if he knew what he was and had his measure.

Was there more than one monster in her

life?

Tacey shook her head. No. But Wystan was waiting in the car, and Rory did need to go home to bed. At least she'd have Wystan to watch over her tonight, or she wouldn't sleep at all. If Matt came to Bell House and set it on fire…

Tacey shivered. No. Matt wouldn't get near Bell House tonight, because Wystan would be keeping watch. Protecting them, they way he always did.

She bade Rochelle and Ben farewell, making them promise to let her know if there was any more trouble at the café, before she grasped Rory's hand and led her out to the car.

"Where's Wystan?" Rory mumbled as she buckled on her seatbelt.

Not in the car, that was for sure. Or anywhere else Tacey could see.

"Wystan? We're going home now. If you want a ride, it's time to go," Tacey said. "Wystan?"

But he didn't appear, and Tacey was forced

to go home without him.

THIRTY-FIVE

"Fire," Tacey said softly, before her mind was engulfed in a wave of panic.

Wystan reacted before he could think. Putting himself between her and the fire, he used his own stone body to smother the flames. A moment later, a flood of icy water cascaded over him, and he heard an ominous crack.

For a moment, he was a boy again, falling

out of a tree he'd climbed with his cousins, when he'd first heard such a cracking sound. For a long moment, the world had felt strange and wrong, but then the pain had hit and he'd known nothing else.

Wystan waited for the pain to overwhelm him now as it had then, but there was nothing. Just a silly gargoyle lying prone on the store room floor, in what should have been a puddle of water, but…wasn't. He hadn't imagined the water, had he?

Tacey held a large metal cylinder with a sort of hose coming out the top, instead of a bucket, like he'd expected. Invisible water? Or water that disappeared after it put the fire out? Or maybe it had all turned to steam? Hard to tell with the amount of smoke in the room.

Tacey found him some replacement clothes, for his own pants had not survived the fire, and helped him dress. Still discombobulated by the fire and the feeling of wrongness, he followed her out into the café, only to stop dead as he realised they were not alone. Rory held tight to the boy Ben's hand, though the boy himself was staring avidly at Wystan.

Before Wystan could warn her, she'd introduced him, and Ben's questions turned pointed.

Wystan needed to get out of there. He mumbled something about needing to clean up, but Tacey wouldn't let him. So he suggested he go out to wait in the car instead, which Tacey did allow.

Only the moment Wystan was out of sight, he slipped inside the nearest wall, and headed out to the courtyard, where the bottle of lamp oil must have come from. The place was empty, but the smell of lamp oil lingered, so he followed it. Through the boarding house, out the front door and around the corner, to where a large, red carriage was parked. No, a car. That's what Tacey called her horseless carriage, though this was a behemoth compared to her phaeton, and it growled like it was a living beast that meant to eat some of the nearby pedestrians for supper.

The growl turned into a roar as the car drove off, and Wystan launched himself into the air to follow…only to plummet back down to the roof when his wings wouldn't hold him. What in heaven's name?

He tore away what remained of his worn shirt, only to discover his wings lay in tatters. Ah, that's what that breaking sound had been – his wings shattering between the onslaught of fire on one side, and ice on the other. Now, after saving Tacey from the fire, he was forced to watch, powerless, as the man who'd put her life in danger sped away.

He did not relish failure, and he looked forward even less to telling Tacey he hadn't caught the culprit. But he was honour bound to tell her, all the same, so he slipped between the walls back to the café, only to find her talking to an unfamiliar man in a police uniform.

No, two of them, saying they would visit the man. Tonight.

Wystan had a chance to redeem himself, to

turn his failure into something better. He would not lose this chance. Instead of confessing to Tacey, he followed the police officers, through the walls of the boarding house as they questioned the receptionist and some of the lodgers, none of whom claimed to have seen anything, before they returned to the watch house, where their vehicle was parked. The police got in, and Wystan leaped lightly onto the roof, then held on tight all the way to the house where the large red car was parked.

The police officers paid the car no heed, merely walking past it to the front door of the grand house, knocking on it as though they had every right to be there, instead of being sent to the servants' entrance, for surely a house as large as this required staff to run it.

Wystan touched the hood of the car, under which he knew the engine lay. Sure enough, it was warm to the touch. This was the same car he'd seen parked around the corner from Tacey's café. The car he'd tried to kill her with.

And the man at the door, waving his hands

as he talked to the police, was most definitely Rory's father. The man she'd begged him to protect her from.

Wystan couldn't hear their conversation from here, so he slipped between the walls of the mansion to creep closer.

"I told you, I've been here all afternoon. I was just about to head out to get takeout for dinner. After the slop they served in prison, I'm still a sucker for a good pizza."

The police officers both stiffened. "You've recently been released from prison?"

The man grinned. "Yeah, don't you watch the news? Terrible miscarriage of justice. When my girlfriend got pregnant to force me into marrying her and I wouldn't, she tried to commit suicide instead, but failed, and framed me for murder instead. The police bought it, the judge and jury bought it, and there I was, an innocent victim, languishing in prison for five long years while the crazy bitch who put me there spent all day drinking coffee with her girlfriends, playing mum to the daughter she tricked me into conceiving and telling lies about me to everyone. I bet that's why you're here, isn't it? Did Tacita tell you I was bothering her? That I did something? Because she's either a really good liar or she's delusional, and either way, hardly a fit mother. I'll be doing her a favour if I take our daughter away from her. Definitely doing the girl a favour. Who knows? Maybe she'll feel so guilty about what she did to me that she'll actually follow through on the suicide this time. Do everybody a favour."

"Mr Masters…"

The police officers stumbled all over each other, a mixture of shock at what he'd said and garbled apologies for what he'd suffered.

What he'd said he suffered…

The man's story was similar enough to Tacey's to suggest there might be some truth in it…yet the details were so vastly different, only one of them could be the truth. If this man was right and Tacey might try to kill herself, then Wystan belonged at her side, where he could protect her. But if Tacey had told the truth and this man had tried to kill her – not just in the past, but tonight at the café – then the greatest danger to her was this man before him. If Wystan kept watch over him, he'd be able to stop him before he could hurt Tacey or Rory.

The man slammed the door, and the police headed back to their car.

Wystan had to choose – go back to Tacey, or stay here?

"Stupid pigs," the man muttered. "They'll believe anything. Pity the café fire didn't kill her. They'd have said something if she was dead, just to see my reaction. Just like last time, when she wouldn't die, either. But that bitch can't be immortal. Her luck's going to run out sometime, and when it does, I'll have the insurance policy to come and collect. I'm coming for you, bitch, because you owe me a big, fat pay check."

Wystan clenched his fists. Of course Tacey had been telling the truth. This bastard had not only tried to kill her in the past, but he wanted to do so even more now. For money, as though he needed it, living in such a grand house. Greedy bastard.

Well, Wystan would just have to change his mind, then. Because if this walloper tried to hurt Rory or Tacey again, Wystan was going to rip his head off. After he tore off his limbs, and any other parts he was particularly attached to. Nobody hurt his family, or at least the one he was sworn to protect.

THIRTY-SIX

The one night she really felt she needed a man's protection, and Wystan wasn't there. She'd gone outside and checked the roof, and she'd even called his name a couple of times from the veranda, but still Tacey got no answer.

Maybe something bad had happened to him. Well, worse than the damage to his wings. Was there a way she could help him fix them? She could hardly call an ambulance – she was pretty sure the local hospitals wouldn't have a clue about treating gargoyles – but if he knew what sort of first aid he needed, at least she'd be able to help.

After the panic of trying to find someone to watch Rory when Mum cancelled, followed by the fiasco of a meeting with the lawyer, not to mention the fire that had nearly burned down the café, the one thing Tacey wanted more than anything right now was someone to give her a hug and tell her everything was going to be all right.

It would probably be a lie, but a good enough hug in a pair of strong arms that pressed her up against a hard, muscled body would be enough to make her believe it. Or at least distract her.

Better yet, a kiss or something more…

Maybe she was crazy, wanting to kiss a monster. Wanting Wystan in her bed. But seeing him lying there on the floor, injured trying to save her, she just couldn't see him as a monster any more. Sure, there were the wings and the horns and the monster size of his…man bits, but he'd never been less than a perfect gentleman around her or Rory. He might look like a monster on the outside…but inside…okay, and maybe some parts on the outside…he was pretty much her ideal man.

And it wasn't that she had anything against wings or horns. The wings could be quite useful and the horns, well…they'd give her something to hold onto if they ever…

Admit it, she told herself. You've wanted that monster cock since the moment you saw it. Hang onto his horns and just ride him until you both screamed.

In fact, if he was in her bedroom right now, that's exactly what she wanted to do. She wanted to screw both their brains out, until she forgot about Matt and lawyers and fires and health inspectors and everything crazy in her life so that for an hour or two, all she did was feel and not think about any of it.

Rory…Rory was safe at home and asleep.

She was both the most stressful and the most important thing in Tacey's life, and Tacey would do anything for her, but in the dark hours of the night when she knew Rory was safe asleep, sometimes she wanted something more. Something for herself. Someone, even. Someone who'd be the responsible one. Who'd take charge so she didn't have to.

Like Wystan had with the fire today.

Did he take charge like that in the bedroom?

She could only hope.

And dream. Fuck, could she dream…

THIRTY-SEVEN

For what seemed like hours, the man watched his television. His took up most of one wall, so much larger than the one in Tacey's house, and the programme was nowhere near as interesting as the ones Tacey and Rory watched. No, the whole time he watched, the screen showed men in tight, bright shirts and pants so short they were barely there at all, running around on a green field, kicking and throwing an egg-shaped ball to one another.

Now, Wystan had played his fair share of games, while at school and occasionally on festival days, but watching other men do so without being part of it? Wystan could not imagine anything more tedious. He would have been in the midst of it, kicking and throwing and tackling and…did that man just bite someone? Ah, that was more like it!

Except that men came rushing onto the field to stop the game and protest about the biting, so Wystan lost interest again.

Which was why he was surprised to hear the clink of keys as the man rose from his seat and headed for the door.

He couldn't leave. At least, not without Wystan coming with him.

So while the man locked the door, Wystan slipped through the walls to the garage, and slid into the back seat of the red car. He stayed low, so the man would not see him in the mirror he knew Tacey liked to check often, and wondered what he should say to try and persuade this man to leave Tacey and Rory alone.

If it had been Effie and the baby, nothing would have kept him away from them. No threat or promise or reasoning of any kind. But Wystan had never wanted Effie dead.

The man threw himself into the driver's seat, and the engine growled into life like the beast it was.

Wystan racked his brain. He was not the silver-tongued speaker among his family. If anyone, that was Grant and Harlow. Grant could talk anyone into anything, while his brother could persuade them out of it. Wystan wished he had both of them here to advise him. But he had only his own wits, and even those seemed to have deserted him.

He was a farmer, and a plain spoken one at that. He could think of only one thing to say, so he slid higher in the seat, so that he would be visible to the driver in his mirror, and addressed him: "What would it take for you to leave Tacey and her daughter alone, Mr

Masters?"

"What the fuck?" Masters stared in the mirror and actually jumped in his seat, before turning right the way around to see Wystan with his own eyes. "What the fuck are you?"

The steering wheel of the car twisted in his hands, but he was heedless of it in his panic at his passenger.

"My name is Wystan Stone, and I'm Miss Bell's gargoyle protector," Wystan said.

"Get the fuck out of my car!" the man shouted, swatting at Wystan.

Wystan easily dodged the flailing hand, though the car's movements had him sliding along the seat. Perhaps Wystan should have fastened his seat belt, like he did in Tacey's care. "Not until you give me your word you will never bother Miss Bell or her daughter again."

It was unlikely he'd get such an assurance from the man right now, who was veering crazily about the road as he tried to reach Wystan. The man had gone quite mad. But

Wystan felt no guilt at all for lying to the man, who had lied so glibly to the police officers about Tacey.

"What the fuck? You're the guy in the suit, aren't you? The one in the video? Get out of my car, or I will fuck you up so bad, you'll need to wear a mask for the rest of your life, no one will want to even look at you!" The man reached back, grabbing Wystan's arm, but in doing so, his car swerved alarmingly toward a concrete wall.

"Mr Masters!" Wystan reached for the steering wheel to correct the car's course, only to find himself fighting the man for control of the car. One moment, they were about to hit the concrete wall, and the next, they were careening toward the metal barrier at the edge of the road. No, the edge of a bridge…

Time seemed to stand still as the car hit the barrier, broadside, but instead of stopping, the car wanted to keep going, flipping up and over until it was no longer on the bridge. Then it began to fall.

Broken glass flew everywhere, from windows that had shattered just like the one this man had broken in the café last night. And then they hit.

It felt as hard as concrete, or another road, until water began to gush into the car as it sank. The man screamed, begging for help and to be let go, but no one was holding him. Blood streaked the water around him, and he just kept on screaming, even as the car sank beneath the surface, and the sound came out more like gurgling.

Wystan heaved himself out of the car's shattered rear window, for the water didn't bother him, as he had no need to breathe. The car settled on the riverbed, so it was a simple matter for him to walk around to the front and peer in at the man.

His eyes were wide open and staring, but unseeing. The dashboard of the car had pinned his legs to the seat, so he hung upside down, his mouth still open as if he wanted to scream one last time.

But he would never scream again. Unless fate saw fit to give him a second chance like the one it had given to Wystan…

No. Effie's death had been tragic. Terrible and perhaps preventable, if the doctor had arrived in time, but not Wystan's fault. Whereas this man had plotted and planned for Tacey's death, which made him a very different creature.

A monster Rory wanted him to protect her from.

And he had. However accidentally, or fortuitously, Wystan had vanquished the monster. Tacey and Rory were safe.

Now, if fate had truly blessed him, he would be allowed to ascend into heaven, to spend eternity with Effie and the baby.

He had only one regret: that he hadn't had a chance to bid Tacey and Rory farewell, and claim a farewell kiss. For he would miss them both sorely.

Wystan closed his eyes, waiting. Surely an angel would come? Or someone?

He waited and he waited, but there were no trumpets, no angels. Not even a devil come to devour him for daring to hope for heaven.

Which meant he still had to protect Tacey and Rory. Hope bloomed in his heart. They still needed him.

Wystan could live with that.

So he turned until he faced downriver, toward the sea, and began to walk along the riverbed home.

THIRTY-EIGHT

"Time to go NOW, Rory!" Tacey shouted. God, she didn't want to be shouting at her, on what might be their last morning together.

If only Matt would drive into a tree or something and not turn up.

Tacey shook her head. No, she shouldn't wish that on Matt, let alone the innocent tree.

A concrete barrier, maybe?

Only if that meant he wouldn't turn up ever.

Because if he turned up late, he'd be even angrier and meaner and he might try to take it out on Rory…

Tacey had packed an overnight bag for Rory, the same one she usually took to Mum's when she stayed overnight, and hidden it in the boot of the car. She wasn't going to surrender Rory to Matt, but he was her father, and entitled to access visits, if nothing else. When he arrived, she was going to tell him Rory could say with him for the weekend, but she had to be home on Sunday afternoon, because she had school on Monday.

He and his arsehole lawyer could try to take her to court, but there were other lawyers in Perth, and she'd find another one. Plus, for every lie Matt had told about her, she could tell just as many stories about him. The police had to find something to link him to the cockroaches or the fire, and she'd bring that to court, too. He couldn't have full custody of Rory if he was in prison for arson, which was a terrible crime in bushfire-prone Perth.

This wasn't the end. She would fight him every step of the way.

As long as they actually made it to the café…

"Rory! I'm going to count to three!"

Rory stomped into view. "I can't find my green thongs."

Probably because they were packed into the overnight bag, Tacey thought but didn't say. "You can't wear those today. It's winter. You need socks and sneakers."

Grumbling, Rory started to pull on her socks.

Tacey wondered how Matt would cope with one of Rory's tantrums. They could be absolutely spectacular, leaving Tacey bone weary, but she knew showing weakness would definitely mean she'd lose, so she had to fight them to the end. Matt…well, he could find that out for himself. If he wanted to be a responsible parent, he wouldn't be getting any help from her.

"Are you ready?" Tacey asked.

Rory started to nod, before her mouth dropped open. "I almost forgot my toy bat! I need to show Uncle Ben!" She raced back to her room.

Tacey sighed. It was going to be a long morning.

THIRTY-NINE

Without Ben or Wystan there, Rory insisted on sitting at Ben's table in the café, beside his growing gallery of art. He'd added comics to the sketches now – all featuring a gargoyle with a cup of coffee in his hand. Were these what he'd been talking about yesterday? Must be, Tacey decided.

She set Rory up with a couple of muffins and a babycino with a stencil of baby Yoda on top in cocoa powder, and began baking up a storm. Saturday mornings were always busy, and she was on her own this morning. Better that no one else had to deal with Matt.

The last batch of cookies came out of the oven just before opening time, so Tacey flipped open the sign and took her place behind the counter.

Coffee after coffee, and muffin after muffin crossed the counter, until the cabinet was almost empty. Tacey dashed into the kitchen for another tray and checked the time. Almost noon! So much for Matt turning up on Saturday morning. He'd never been punctual before, so at least that hadn't changed.

For a moment, she dared to hope he wasn't coming, but she drove that thought away a moment after she'd had it. No, if Matt said he'd be here, he'd be here, even if he was late. He always kept his promises, especially the dark ones.

Noon came and went, so Tacey made a sandwich for Rory, setting a salad alongside it that was more cherry tomatoes than lettuce. As long as she ate some veggies, she was doing okay, wasn't she?

When the lunch rush was over, Tacey took a moment to grab a sandwich for herself. She'd put extra brie in one of the turkey ones, and hidden it in the fridge with the milk. No wonder these sold so well. It was delicious. She should make these a permanent menu item.

Of course, the moment her mouth was full, customers walked in. No, two police officers.

"Do you have any news about the lab tests? Or did he confess to the firebomb?" she asked eagerly.

The two officers looked at each other in confusion before one of them shook her head.

Only then did Tacey realise that neither of them were the same officers who'd come after the fire.

"Are you Tacita Bell?" the female officer asked.

Tacey nodded. "Call me Tacey," she said.

"Do you know a man named Matthew

Masters?" the officer asked.

Again, Tacey nodded. "He's my daughter's father. He said…he said he'd be here this morning to pick her up. He's demanding full custody of her, but she barely knows him. Until a court orders otherwise, the best he's going to get is access visits."

"Your daughter is Aurora Bell?"

Tacey pointed at Ben's table. "That's her over there." She winced as Rory bit into a tomato and juice squirted across her cheek.

"When did you last see Mr Masters?"

Well, she hadn't actually seen him throw the Molotov cocktail or the bag of cockroaches. "Maybe two weeks ago, here in the café."

"Did he seem down to you at all?"

Tacey laughed. "He seemed bullying and threatening. He told me he was going to take our daughter from me and that if I knew what was good for me, I'd come along, too. Like I'm stupid enough to go back to a man who tried to kill me."

"Do you know where he is now?"

Tacey only laughed harder. "He's supposed to be here, so, nope, I have no idea where he could be that's more important than the daughter he hasn't cared about until now, when he suddenly wants her. Maybe he came to his senses and decided to sell his parents' fancy house and go live off the proceeds on a beach in Bali?" If the borders were open, which of course they weren't.

The two cops exchanged a heavy glance.

Tacey's heart sank. Whatever they knew that she didn't, it wasn't good.

She wet her lips. "Is it my house? Did he burn down Bell House?"

A long moment passed, before the male one said, "Miss Bell, Mr Masters drove off the Mount Henry Bridge last night. From what we can determine from the traffic cameras, he was driving erratically, nearly hitting several other cars and the concrete barrier, before he suddenly swerved and drove off the bridge. We found his body in the river this morning."

Tacey could barely believe it. Sure, she'd

thought about something bad happening to Matt, but she hadn't seriously considered… "Matt's dead?"

Both of them nodded. "And we believe your daughter is his sole heir."

Rory owned Matt's parents' mansion in Salter Point? Christine's pristine lawns? Oh, Christine would roll over in her grave if she knew.

"Rory's too young to be owning property. She's only just started to learn to read, and certainly not well enough to be signing contracts any time soon."

The male officer coughed. "Well, as her legal guardian, you'd be responsible for things until she turns eighteen. Of course, the lawyers have to go through all the paperwork, which might take months, but when it's all sorted, I think you'll find that before Mr Masters tragically took his own life, he knew his daughter would be provided for."

Matt? Suicide? Never. Driving drunk or on his phone and not paying attention to the road, maybe. But whatever had made Matt drive off that bridge, for her and Rory, it was more like a miracle.

"Thank you for letting me know. Can I get you a coffee, or a muffin, maybe?" Tacey offered.

The police officers declined, then left, with a promise that Matt's lawyer would be in touch. Oh, Tacey was really looking forward to that meeting. Dominic Lamont was going to kiss her arse.

FORTY

The rest of the day went by in a blur. Customers came and went, and Octavia wanted to work on her super secret project upstairs tonight, so she'd offered to man the counter until the café closed, so when the sunset streaked the sky orange, Tacey hung up her apron, and took Rory home.

They stopped for pizza on the way, so the house was dark by the time they arrived. The security lights on the veranda activated as soon as they pulled up, revealing a shadowy form sitting in the chair beside the door.

A huge, hulking shadow.

Tacey's heart leaped, but Rory got there first.

"Mr Monster!" she cried, leaping out of the car to run to Wystan.

Tacey followed at a slower pace, carrying the pizza box, but she was in time to hear Wystan say, "It's all right, you're safe now, Miss Rory. The monster can't hurt you ever again."

He knew Matt was dead.

Which he couldn't possibly know unless he'd been in the café when the police came, or if he'd been responsible for it.

But Tacey couldn't ask him that in front of Rory.

"You should come in," she told him instead, leading the way.

"What about the rule about no monsters allowed in the house?" Wystan asked.

Tacey took a deep breath. "That only applies to monsters who might want to harm us. Are you a danger to Rory and me?"

Wystan shook his head. "I'm sworn to protect you, now and always."

Which didn't explain why he'd been missing when she needed him most, unless he'd been with Matt. Killing Matt.

"Then you can come in."

Rory cheered, grabbing Wystan's hand to pull him through the door. If she knew he'd actually killed a man for her, Rory wouldn't be so trusting.

Then again, he might not have done it. Matt really might have killed himself, however accidentally. But Tacey didn't believe it.

Rory couldn't go to bed soon enough.

FORTY-ONE

"G'night, Mr Monster!" Rory wrapped her arms around Wystan's neck and hugged him tight enough to strangle him, if he'd needed to breathe. Then she kissed his cheek, before running off.

Tacey just watched, not saying a word, but her eyes said plenty.

They said if he didn't tell her everything, she'd kick him out of the house. For good this time.

Eternity as a gargoyle on her roof. Well, there were worse ways to keep watch. But he could live with that, if that was what she wanted. At least he'd know she was safe, and Rory, too.

Finally, she closed the door to Rory's bedroom and took a chair on the opposite side of the table from him. Then she folded her arms, fixing her gaze on him, and said, "Explain."

And he did. Lying about going to the car, trying to chase after Masters, riding on top of the police car, hearing the man's plans for Tacey, before sneaking into the back seat of his car to try to persuade him to leave Tacey alone.

"I didn't expect him to go crazy. The car just flipped and we were in the water and he was screaming and then…it was all over," Wystan finished.

Tacey had the strangest expression on her face. Like she was trying not to smile, but her face kept wanting to anyway. Finally, she said, "So…you're telling me Matt's death was an accident. He freaked out when he saw you, lost control of the car, and got himself killed in a car accident. Just like he intended to happen to me, only he drove off a bridge, instead of over a cliff."

Wystan nodded. He'd seen the similarities, too. Perhaps this was justice, served by a fate that didn't like lawyers.

Tacey rose hesitantly to her feet, then held out her arms. "I believe I need to thank you."

Used to Rory's exuberant hugs, he knew Tacey was offering something similar, but she was no innocent child.

"You don't owe me anything. I'm your sworn protector. You summoned me, remember?" he said.

"Will you just hug me already? I feel stupid standing here with my arms up, if you don't."

He had to laugh at that. Nor could he disobey a command, even if he'd wanted to.

She felt soft and delicate in his arms, though

he knew she was easily as strong as he was, when it counted. Oh, but the delight of her breasts against his chest! He hadn't been this close to a woman since…

"Now kiss me."

FORTY-TWO

Tacey thought she'd remembered that first kiss, but her memories hadn't done it or Wystan justice. He kissed like she was a drink in the desert, when he was dying of thirst, searing her insides all the way down to her core.

Only now did she realise that he wasn't wearing any pants, and the monster jutting from his groin was hot and hard against her belly.

Tacey took a split second to remember that Octavia was at the café, Callie was still at that wedding and Rory was asleep in her room. Tomorrow, they'd have a full house again. If she was being sensible, she should take him to her bedroom before they did anything, but right now, she was sick of being sensible.

She wanted to ride that monster cock until she screamed.

Tacey pushed Wystan down onto the nearest chair, then dragged her shirt over her head. Her pants hit the floor, followed by her underwear. She took a deep breath, before she straddled his lap.

Even the head of his cock felt huge, but she didn't hesitate. She guided him inside her, sinking down, down that enormous length, until she felt fuller than she'd ever been before.

"Oh, Miss Tacey, you are divine," Wystan groaned. "Are you sure you want this?"

Tacey laughed. "I've never wanted anything more."

And then she rode him. Hard. Until the first orgasm sent her reeling, quickly followed by a second, and a third.

Any more and she'd fall apart, unable to walk. If it wasn't too late for that already.

Wystan rose from his seat, still deep inside her, and she wrapped her legs around his waist to keep him there. "I'm taking you to bed, Miss Tacey."

"Good."

It was only a few steps, but every one made him rub against her, so she was on the cusp of another orgasm by the time he set her gently on her bed.

"Would you like me to stand watch on the roof while you sleep?" Wystan asked, for all the world like he wasn't buried balls deep inside her, exactly where she wanted him. Now, and every other night. She didn't want a cold stone sentinel on the roof.

"No," she breathed, lifting her hips in an effort to get him to finish what he'd started. She was so close. "I want…I want…you. In my bed, like this, all night. Every night."

"Are you sure?" he asked, slowly pulling almost out of her, before easing deep inside in the most tortuously glacial thrust only a man made of stone could possibly manage.

"Yes. Please, Wystan." She almost didn't recognise her own voice, breathy and begging. "More, please!"

And, being the monster he was, or maybe because he wasn't, he gave her exactly what she asked for. Over and over and over again.

ABOUT THE AUTHOR

Demelza Carlton has always loved the ocean, but on her first snorkelling trip she found she was afraid of fish.

She has since swum with sea lions, sharks and sea cucumbers and stood on spray drenched cliffs over a seething sea as a seven-metre cyclonic swell surged in, shattering a shipwreck below.

Demelza now lives in Perth, Western Australia, the shark attack capital of the world.

The *Ocean's Gift* series was her first foray into fiction, followed by her suspense thriller *Nightmares* trilogy. She swears the *Mel Goes to Hell* series ambushed her on a crowded train and wouldn't leave her alone.

Want to know more? You can follow Demelza on Facebook, Twitter, YouTube or her website, Demelza Carlton's Place at:

www.demelzacarlton.com

More Books by Demelza Carlton

<u>**Colony: Aqua series**</u>

Halcyon (#1)

Poseidon (#2)

Apollo (#3)

Colony: Nyx series

Fang (#1)

Talon (#2)

Claw (#3)

<u>**Siren of Secrets series**</u>

Ocean's Secret (#1)

Ocean's Gift (#2)

Ocean's Infiltrator (#3)

<u>**Siren of War series**</u>

Ocean's Justice (#1)

Ocean's Widow (#2)

Ocean's Bride (#3)

Ocean's Rise (#4)

Ocean's War (#5)

How To Catch Crabs

<u>**Nightmares Trilogy**</u>

Nightmares of Caitlin Lockyer (#1)

Necessary Evil of Nathan Miller (#2)

Afterlife of Alana Miller (#3)

<u>**Romance Island Resort series**</u>

Maid for the Rock Star (#1)

The Rock Star's Email Order Bride (#2)

The Rock Star's Virginity (#3)

The Rock Star and the Billionaire (#4)

The Rock Star Wants A Wife (#5)

The Rock Star's Wedding (#6)

Maid for the South Pole (#7)

Romance a Medieval Fairytale series

Enchant: Beauty and the Beast Retold

Dance: Cinderella Retold

Fly: Goose Girl Retold

Revel: Twelve Dancing Princesses
Retold

Silence: Little Mermaid Retold

Awaken: Sleeping Beauty Retold

Embellish: Brave Little Tailor Retold

Appease: Princess and the Pea Retold

Blow: Three Little Pigs Retold

Return: Hansel and Gretel Retold

Wish: Aladdin Retold

Melt: Snow Queen Retold

Spin: Rumpelstiltskin Retold

Kiss: Frog Prince Retold

Reflect: Snow White Retold

Roar: Goldilocks Retold

Cobble: Elves and the Shoemaker Retold

Float: Enchanted Horse Retold

Steal: Forty Thieves Retold

Call: Pied Piper Retold

Fall: Scheherazade Retold

Feather: Swan Maidens Retold

Cross: Billy Goats Gruff Retold

Weave: Rapunzel Retold

Claim: Puss in Boots Retold

Curse: Rose Red Retold

Cross: Three Billy Goats Gruff Retold

Weave: Rapunzel Retold

Claim: Puss in Boots Retold

<u>**Heart of Stone series**</u>

Heart of Steel (#0)

Broken Chains (#1)

Broken Bonds (#2)

Broken Dreams (#3)